Death Scent

A Jessica Anderson
K-9 Mystery

by D. L. Keur

Death Scent

A Jessica Anderson K-9 Mystery

by D. L. Keur

Published by D. L. Keur, Sandpoint, ID 83864

Dedication

To Bailey, my wonder mutt,

To my dad,

And to Laura Belgrave, who made me do it.

Acknowledgements

Huge thanks to my editors, Anita Lewis, Marva Dasef, and Laura Belgrave. Without them, this book would be 'less than'. Thanks to Ann Davis, Mitch's mom, for her enthusiasm, support, and photos. Photo credits go to: Ann Davis, Artem Ivanchencko (unsplash.com), Fabrizio Conti (unsplash.com), and kuzmaphoto (shutterstock.com). Also to my German linguistics helper who insists she not be mentioned by name.

Copyright

First Edition

ISBN: 9798740366210

Orders, inquiries, and correspondence should be addressed to: D. L. Keur &/or F. W. Lineberry, P. O. Box 2419, Sandpoint, ID 83864

Authorship, design and formatting by D. L. Keur, www.DLKeur.com

Cover art by D. L. Keur, www.zentao.com

Printed in the United States of America

Table of Contents

Death Scent

A Jessica Anderson
K-9 Mystery

by D. L. Keur

D. L. Keur

1 – 9-1-1 Call

OSO, JESSIE'S QUIET, very independent Elkhound, watched from a distance, reserving judgment.

Giant Milo, the Wonder Mutt, lay in a crouched 'down' position, still and sphinx-like, except for his tail, which tentatively brushed back and forth in the grass. Like Oso, Milo was reserving judgment, but with his natural optimism.

Jessica Anderson touched the 'on' icon on the interface open on her laptop. The two little machines sitting on the ground in front of her clicked a couple of times, lights on them blinking.

All three German Shepherds—Acer, Britta, and Sumi—pricked their ears. The fur on their backs rippled a bit, while Mitch, the Marvelous, Jessie's young Belgian Malinois, came instantly to his feet. He tipped his head sideways, his attention riveted.

Predictably, her top ground tracking dog, a deep copper-colored Irish Setter cross named Queenie, bounded up to the little machines, stopped short, backed up, barked, then moved in closer. One sniff, and she took off to race around the field in deliciously happy circles. Queenie thought them some new game or toy …which, in a way, they were. …And weren't. "Good dogs," Jessie crooned.

All the dogs relaxed. Momentarily. Then all of them stood and went to full attention. The German Shepherds, or, as Jessie thought of them, GSDs, raised their hackles. So did Mitch as the drones came alive, the machines unfolding like strange insects as they engaged their tiny rotors to pull themselves aloft.

Only Oso and Milo were still open to the possibility that these weren't 'danger'. Only Queenie still thought them marvelous fun.

"*Good* dogs, *gute Hunde, brave Hunde*," Jessie called again, using both English and German to sooth her pack as the machines moved higher, hovered for a moment, then flew outward, following the path that Jessie had previously programmed into the software's control interface. "It's okay. They're good guys," Jessie said to the dogs. "They're going to save us a lot of time and effort." At least, she hoped they would. Today would test that possibility.

Almost as one, the dogs looked back to her, and she smiled—her pack, The Motley Mutts, as her grandfather called them, and she was their pack leader. "Good dogs. *Brave Hunde*," she answered them, English for her rescues, Queenie, Milo, Mitch, and Oso, German for the Shepherds, though, because of her constant use, all of them knew both lingos, now.

Watching her new tools circle the field twice, her dogs' every sense tracking them, Jessie was pleased to see the machines were following her programming exactly. She grinned, then touched in the second part of the program, one that would send the drones out to do a test search. *This will save countless search hours for us. If we can just get Idaho to relax their privacy laws a little.* Still, there were other states. Jessie wasn't limited to state lines, not now. Not with canine search and rescue expert Callen Parker on her side, and, so far, he was.

The all but silent machines disappeared in the distance, heading toward Long Peak. Jessie hoped she'd gotten all the parameters right. These were a lot better than the toys she'd been practicing with, but this was their first test flight, and, at five grand apiece, she didn't want them flying into a tree or a cliff, thanks. But she'd already tested their proximity sensors, and they seemed to be working fine. Still, though, she'd set the program to keep their altitude above the treetops and the Cliffs of Long.

Watching her laptop intently, she kept an eye on both their audio-visual feeds and their GPS positions on her screen. So far, so good. They were half a mile out already. "They're fast," she whispered to herself.

A dog whined—Britta. "*Braves Mädchen, ganz braves Mädchen,*" she said soothingly. Acer touched his nose to his friend, and Britta yawned once, then lay down with a groan, Acer squatting down to sit next to her, hip to hip.

On her screen, the GPS locators were showing the little flying bots now a mile out and still absolutely locked to their programmed flight path on her test search grid. She turned on the motion sensors just to see what they would do, and if they actually functioned the way the company said they would, sticking to the search grid and avoiding each other, but reporting movement.

Within moments, one reported in—what looked like maybe a raven taking flight. The camera adjusted its focus, and the bird came crisply into view before disappearing into the trees. The drone stayed true to its programming, maintaining flight path.

They were amazing, and so was the software that controlled them. Not as amazing as her dogs, but Jessie was glad she'd come across the company responsible for building them—a small firm located in Alaska. They were fast, light, and had twice the flight time of comparably equipped drones. They were also more fragile, but the software helped with the flying.

At two miles out, some eight minutes into their weaving, criss-cross search pattern, Jessica caught sight of something the wrong shape and color on the mountain's broken snow floor. Taking manual control of the drone nearest to it, she lowered altitude and set the camera to target the object.

With sudden recognition of what it was, she zoomed in. A proximity sensor blinked. Her other drone avoided collision all on its own and was now crossing to the east of the one she manually flew. It reported movement.

Diverted, she let the one she controlled hover on auto-pilot, hoping it caught movement from the body, while she turned her attention to what the other was reporting—another person, she realized. That person disappeared into the woods, but the drone still sensed it. She gave it autonomous control and watched, riveted, as the machine now dodged between trees, self-navigating on proximity sensors and its software's AI. *Be careful*, she pleaded silently to the little flying robot.

A flash of red.... The camera zoomed and focused. The drone dodged and shifted, changing angles to auto-orient. The flash of red reappeared—the backend of a pickup about fifty yards ahead, part of the vehicle occluded by the trees. What she could see was that its tailgate was up, said 'Chevrolet', and it had no rear license plate. Jessie keyed the drone to hover. There was the sound of the engine starting. Then, the vehicle disappeared from sight.

Jessie touched in a command for the drone to raise altitude to above tree level again and seek previous target. "In for a dime, in for five grand," she muttered, hoping the drone's proximity sensors accurately could sense overhanging branches above itself. A dog whine answered her, but she kept her concentration on the screen, which had gone to a blur.

Shifting her attention to the other drone's feed, she saw that, at least as much as she could tell, the body hadn't moved. Asleep, injured, or dead, she wondered.

And, deciding, she dropped the drone down close to investigate and saw what she didn't want to.

Every dog came to full alert, their eyes riveted on her.

*

"9-1-1, WHAT IS YOUR EMERGENCY?"

Stick to basics: "My name is Jessie Anderson. There's a person lying on the bank of the creek up on Long Peak about two-point-two miles north by northeast of Anderson Working Dogs' northwest property corner marker. They're not moving."

The woman on the other end of the call was silent for a second, then said the predictable: "Stay on the line with me, please, Jessie."

"Yes, Ma'am."

Eyes glued on her drone's feeds, she heard the woman call code. From the corner of her eye, she watched her dogs 'talk' to one another, then, as if one, move to surround her.

The drone tracking the red truck displayed it driving out of the woods, then heading down the old Forest Service road. The drone kept the vehicle in focus as it

"Boss?"

Landon looked up to see Lieutenant Pete 'Red' Wheeler's head poked around his open door. "Yes, Lieutenant?"

"We've got a weird one."

Landon didn't like the look on Red's face. "What is it?"

"The Anderson kid called in a body."

What Anderson kid? They all flew the coop years ago. ...Unless somebody had a baby nobody had told him about. Then, when the rest sank in, he frowned. "A body?"

"Yep. Dispatch has sent deputies, and Barry's out there, too, but, well, I thought you ought to know."

His third-in-command had gone out—serious, then. Landon closed the lid on his laptop, got his piece out of the lockup in his bottom drawer, and secured his desk. "Let's go. And, Red? I want you out there."

"Yes, sir."

*

DOGS TRAILING, Jessie poked her head around the corner of the doorway. "Dad?"

Oli Anderson looked up. "What's up, Jessie?"

She shook her head. 'What's up' meant he saw that she was troubled, though how he always knew puzzled her.

Letting out a breath she hadn't realized she was holding, she stepped in, Milo leading, Mitch who was half his size, glued shoulder to leg with him. Next to her, Acer stayed at her left knee, with Britta on the right, and the other three, Sumi, Oso, and Queenie, just behind. "I think I just screwed up."

Her father sat back, and, stretching out his long frame, waved her toward a chair. "Sit down. Talk to me, my Jess."

Letting out another big breath, she plopped herself down in one of the overstuffed leather chairs across from him, the dogs lying down around her. "You know I got my drones in yesterday, right?"

He chuckled and nodded. "Ye-eah."

"Well, I sent them out on a test flight this morning."

His blue eyes twinkled, and he smiled. "Ye-eah, you told me you were going to."

Jessie felt her face screw up and schooled herself back to normal. "Well, they caught somebody on public land, somebody not moving, and somebody else beating feet out of there. It didn't look right."

Her dad—big, formidable, and rock hard—sat up and forward. Oli's eyes went suddenly sharper blue.

Acer pushed himself up from a down into a sit, his eyes intent on the man who had trained him. Britta did the same almost simultaneously. Mitch stood up, then sat. Milo stayed in sphinx mode, watching intently, his tail still, its tip lifted. Queenie, Oso, and Sumi came alert, too, their ears pricked sharply, their bodies almost rigid in their 'down's.

"Go on," her father said.

"I shouldn't have, but I dialed 9-1-1 and reported it."

Her dad's forehead crinkled. "Why shouldn't you have? It's what you *should* have done. What's the problem?"

"The drones."

"You have all your licenses, right?"

"Yes."

"You cross over somebody's land you don't have permission yet to fly over?"

"No."

He frowned. "Then, what?"

"They're going to want to take them, and my external drives, my laptop, and probably my desktop, too. Then they'll log them into evidence, and I won't see them forever, *if* ever." ...And it was his money that had bought half of that equipment, which, of course, he already knew, since he'd loaned it to her.

"Who is 'they', and why would they confiscate your equipment?"

"Probably the Sheriff's Office. And because of the laws concerning digital evidence authenticity and chain of custody rules for evidence."

"They can't take them unless you allow them to, not without a warrant."

"Yeah. I know, but...."

Oli shook his head and sat back, relaxing again. "You know better than me what you have to do to prevent that from happening."

"Yeah. But they may consider me 'uncooperative' if I stop them."

"Then let them consider you uncooperative. That's what? Ten grand worth of equipment?"

"Twenty, at least."

"Right." Oli gave her a gentle smile. "Is the person okay?"

"Dead, I think. There's evidence of livor mortis." Then, at his questioning look, she added, "Her—it looks like a her, anyway.... The body's blood has pooled—gravity."

Her dad's face went to that blank, neutral look that Jessie had never really understood, but happened any time there was trouble.

Acer and Britta stood up. So did Mitch. Milo's stature seemed to grow taller and stiller, if that was possible. His tail curved up in a stiffened arc. Queenie, Oso, and Sumi came to their feet, as well, and Queenie gave a little whine.

Running his fingers through his hair, Oli blew out a huge breath, sat up straight, picked up the phone, and hit one of the quick dial buttons on it.

***

3 – Pertinents

THE RADIO CRACKLED, then Dispatch came on. "We have a definite 10-84 on the south slope of Long Peak, Sheriff. Do you copy?"

"Copy," he responded. "10-3."

"10-4," came back, the voice saying it obviously disgruntled. "…Out."

One of these days he was going to break some heads. What was so hard about using the new computer system? It certainly was more trustworthy than the radio with all the dropouts in the county. So were cell phones, now …though, admittedly, not so much where he was headed. Heck, nothing but smoke signals worked up there unless you got up on a ridge.

Neither Dispatch nor his deputies were compliant with his new directive, though. They just didn't get it, that ears were listening and knew the ten codes. Or they didn't want to get it, maybe. All of them were his dad's hand-picked men and women—good officers, but stubborn, too.

His irritation began evaporating. It wasn't *that* big a deal, really. Not much happened here—not usually. A few lost hikers and hunters, bar fights, vehicle mishaps—that sort of thing. Rarely did they get a homicide.

Landon wondered what had happened this time. Was it really a homicide? He would have been told if it was a knife or gunshot victim. *So, it's probably an accident, not homicide. Probably due to a fall.* ...But the south slope of Long Peak wasn't that steep or treacherous, except near the Upper and Lower Long Cliff Falls and The Cliffs of Long, not like the north side.

He sighed. There was still some snow and ice up there, though, especially ice, despite an unusually warm end of March and first week in April with the flooding that brought. And it was rocky up on Long Peak and still way below freezing at night.

An early season hiker slipping on creek ice? Cracked their skull open was his guess. Still, his sixth sense told him he needed help on this one. Better call now while he still had bars.

Touching a button on his steering wheel, he tried Boise and Nampa first because that was the best expediency, then, on their begging off, made a call to

Crime Scene Investigator Wilber Schmidt up in Coeur d'Alene.

*

LAWYERS HAD NEVER BEEN HIGH on Jessie's preferred list of people with whom to associate until her father's spoke to her on speakerphone. The man quizzed her about what she'd told the 9-1-1 operator, then he told her exactly what she had to do—lock down everything. "It won't stop them if they have a warrant, but you don't have to make it easy for them."

Should the sheriff request access to viewing the originals, she was to comply. She was not, under any circumstances, to allow anyone to remove her property, "not without a warrant." Instead, she was to burn a copy of the material to a thumb drive and allow the officer to take that copy. Only. And she was to admit nothing. "Stick to the facts that are public record—what you told the 9-1-1 operator. Meanwhile, I know the judge who the sheriff usually taps for warrants. I'll give him a call. I'm going to make this a little harder for them."

Jessie did as she'd been instructed, her dad watching from the doorway of her office as six of her seven dogs lay variously placed in the large room, watching them both. Except for Acer. He stuck like glue to Jessie's left knee.

Done cabling her laptop to the desk and locking up the drones and all her external drives, she turned to her dad. "That's the best I can do," she said.

Oli nodded. "Let's go let your grandparents know what's coming down."

Six dogs stood up. Acer's ears snapped forward. "*Platz*." she said. All seven lay down.

"Best bring your dogs to the house, Jessie. Just in case the sheriff comes barreling in here."

All seven dogs stood up, again.

"Okay."

*

"IT'S SUE BIGSBY. I recognize her," Captain Barry Olmstead told Reid when he got there. Seeing the body, Landon recognized her, too, even though she was face down on the snow and rocks, her pink-and-white dyed hair fallen over her face.

"She works ...worked morning shift at The Club Café," Barry added. "She's been dead a bit, though. Cold. No rigor mortis. Got photos, already. Medical Examiner is on his way."

"We're not moving that body, yet. Cancel the ME until tomorrow. I've got Wilbur flying in from Coeur d'Alene," Landon growled.

"You *did* call, then."

"Yep. Flying himself in. Boise and Nampa are too buried in work."

"Not surprised. It's a mess down there."

Landon grunted. Yeah, he watched the news, too.

"Glad it's Wilber," Barry came back.

"Yeah."

"Perimeter is set up, not that we need one way up here with the mountain goats."

"Grizzlies, too," Red Wheeler muttered.

"There's that, yeah," Barry admitted. "Called in some reserve deputies to man it, but, since you brought Red, I'd like him here to supervise. Don't get many like this in our neck of the woods. We're all kind of green at things like this."

"You're right."

"What now?"

"Barry, I want you to head into town to get me the search warrant I've ordered from Judge Peterson."

Red frowned. "Who's the warrant for?"

"One Jessica Marie Anderson."

Red looked surprised. "The dog girl?"

Sheriff Landon Reid drove a look at him. "Why do you call her that?"

"She's an Anderson, was in my graduating class, and everyone called her that."

Irritation rose again. "I know *who* she is. I was in high school, too, remember?" Nobody would forget look-alike twins with platinum blonde hair—*Can you say white?*—one of them always in your face and the other one always trying to dodge you. "What I asked is why you called her 'the dog girl'. It sounds …*rude*."

Shrugging, Red said, "It's just something we called Jessie as kids because of her dad and granddad, and because, well, she was always the winner in 4H—best in dog obedience, in agility, in utility—you name it."

"Hmmph. Wasn't in 4H myself," Landon muttered.

"Yeah. I know. You were all FFA and high school rodeo." Then, "I was in high school, too, remember?"

Reid took the chide. He deserved it.

Barry Olmstead was back snapping more pictures around the body. "Barry? Give that over to Red here to finish up. I need you to get going. I want to secure whatever evidence the woman has before she has time for second thoughts. I'll meet you at the Andersons."

"Yes, sir."

Back in his unit, Landon was amazed to find that both the onboard computer and his phone had signal. *Look at that. Way up here.* That was new. Maybe the county commissioners had made an impact with the telecommunications company, after all. Reid sat pondering that miracle as Barry turned around, then headed down the mountain. His computer came to life moments later, and what came through was his requested background check on Miss Jessica Marie Anderson. That it had come in this fast meant that it was already in the system, so she was either a felon—not according to her driver's license application—or had applied recently for some job that called for one.

He paused the feed and started reading. Shook his head and decided to wait till the full background check loaded into the machine. When it was finally done, he paged through the pertinents, scanning the highlights. Seven minutes later, satisfied that he knew enough, he headed down the mountain toward the turnoff to the Anderson place.

He clocked the miles. He clocked the time it took to make the drive. And he thought.

This woman—someone he vividly remembered from his junior and senior years in high school—was now a full-fledged and certified criminal science investigator or CSI. She had been a sworn officer with the Blaine County Sheriff's Office, had been injured in the line of duty, and left the force—Post Traumatic Stress Disorder—PTSD—they said. She was now domiciled at her family's place.

He shook his head. He would have never, *ever* guessed Jessica Anderson to have gone into law enforcement—never in a million years. She just wasn't the type. Yet, there it was on his screen.

He hissed a whistle through his teeth. *Never in a million years! Something's off.*

***

4 – Idaho Code

KEEPING ONE EYE on the drive, her dogs stationed around her, Jessie began to relate what was happening to her grandparents. She blessed the fact that her dad broke in and did most of the explaining when her granddad's face turned into a storm. At that, Acer stiffened, and Jessie reached a hand down to touch his ruff. He relaxed a bit, but, throughout the rest of the discussion, as her Granddad Darby kept his eyes glued on her, a frown crinkling his brow, Acer kept his attention focused on Darby. She kept telling herself to breathe as Darby's eyes kept staring. She kept stroking Acer's ruff.

"I think someone's coming up the drive," Jessie's soft-voiced grandmother, Ana-Mari, said.

Her dad stood up. So did Jessie and her pack. "Let's get this over with." He glanced around the table. "After, we're all going out to dinner at The Hereford. That okay with you, Mom?"

"Yes," Ana-Mari replied, her warm hazel eyes smiling. "We've not started preparing anything for dinner, yet."

"Good. The Hereford it is, then."

Outside, an SUV with the word 'SHERIFF' painted on its side pulled into the working dog building's diagonal parking area, idled for a moment, then went still. A man about as tall as her dad, but a little lankier, got out. He was wearing a white Stetson, or, more correctly, a silver one. *That hat has to be at least a 100x. How many beaver gave their lives for that vanity?* And then there were his boots, also top of the line.

With a start, when her eyes finally settled on his face—a pockmarked face she recognized—she realized she knew him …had had a crush on him in high school, just like everybody else. She backed a step. Her dogs, almost as one, rose from sitting to standing as Jessie felt her dad's hand touch her back. "It's okay, Jessie," Oli said softly.

"Good afternoon. I'm Sheriff Landon Reid."

Like I don't know that already.

The man eyed her. The dogs eyed him. Jessie held her breath, but there was no recognition there, and Jessica blessed the fact that she'd been far beneath his sights in high school—a nobody to a somebody. It was something she'd been just as glad of then as she was now. "You're Miss Jessica Anderson?" he asked.

"Yes-ss—." Of habit, Jessie'd almost said 'sir', but she caught herself. She was a civilian, and that distinction, especially now, needed to be maintained. Knowing how law enforcement worked, she had no doubt that Landon Reid already had secured a background check on her. He already knew all about her. Probably her whole family.

"Do you have I.D.?"

"Yes, sir." And, there it was, that ingrained habit. So much for maintaining autonomy.

"May I see it?"

Jessie nodded. Dogs trailing, she retrieved her wallet from her Suburban, opened it, pulled out her driver's license, and handed it to him.

He glanced at it, glanced at her, grunted, then handed it back. "And you called 9-1-1 about finding a dead body near Long Creek?"

"No. Through my drones' feeds, I viewed a prone body laying on the bank of Long Creek on National Forest land about two-point-two miles north by northeast of this property's northwest section corner."

"Did you attempt to communicate with the victim or go to the victim's location?"

"No. I didn't know the person was a victim when my drone picked them up on its feed. They could have been asleep. But I also didn't know if maybe they were hurt or dead. I dialed 9-1-1."

"Why didn't you attempt to go and check?"

"Because the location is remote, and it would take about forty-five minutes to reach that position by road or horseback from here, which I know from experience is out of cell range. Further," and, again, Jessie had to stop herself from saying 'sir', "I was instructed to stay on the phone by the 9-1-1 operator."

During the whole exchange, the dogs' and her dad's heads tracked from one speaker—the sheriff—to the other—her. If the situation hadn't been so serious, it would have been something Jessie would have loved to video.

At her last response, Sheriff Reid grunted and tapped something down on his phone. "Do you still have those drone feeds?"

"Yes."

"May I see them?"

"Yes." Jessie handed him the thumb drive.

"I'd like to see the originals, please."

Jessie eyed her dad. He nodded. "Okay. This way," and, as a unit, they all headed toward her building, her pack splitting up to do escort, flanking, and rear guard duty. Luckily, the sheriff didn't seem to even notice. But Jessie and her dad both did. Jessie saw Oli smile his secret, gleeful smirk.

Inside her office, she saw Reid eye her drones, now locked away in a glass-faced cabinet. *Here it comes.*

"Are those your drones?"

"They are." She asked the dogs to park themselves on the far side of the room. All but Acer complied. Acer was having none of it. He stayed nailed to her side.

Sitting down at her desk and logging into her laptop, Jessie brought up the drone feeds—both of them—then got up. "There you go, Sheriff. Just hit the enter key, and they'll play."

Jessie motioned her dad to sit down in the only other chair, then pulled up a piece of floor for herself, sitting herself cross-legged in a position where she could watch the computer screen, too, Acer sitting, not downing, beside her. And she felt suddenly exposed without all her dogs coming to snuggle in beside her. On a whim, she signaled, and, quietly, all of them came and surrounded her—her warm, furred family.

By the time she felt safe, Reid was already deep into the logs that mapped computer activity. That surprised her. He was computer savvy. But not that computer savvy, it seemed. He needed her help to get back to the drone recordings. She verbally talked him through it, unwilling to leave the happy comfort provided by her canine buddies.

The sheriff watched the entirety of the two drone feeds, her dad pulling his chair closer to watch them, too—thirty minutes for one, and thirty-two for the other one. By the time the videos were finally over, Jessie's butt was numb from sitting still on the cold, hard floor. *I should get carpet. This isn't comfortable for the dogs, either. Or maybe just some more dog rugs.* It was something to think about.

Reid glanced her way for just a moment, then closed out the windows on the screen and sat back. His hand fingered the cable lock on the laptop. Then, he chuckled. Jessie found the sound ominous. So did the dogs. All of them sat up, and Jessie whispered to them for calm.

Outside, her dad's dogs went off, and Reid swiveled the chair as Jessie's father began to rise. "That's just one of my deputies bringing a search warrant," Reid said. He grinned as he said it, and that disturbed her. Abruptly, he turned his face back to Jessie. "I have a question for you, Miss Anderson, one which I don't expect you to answer, but here it is: Were you subpoenaed for deposition and/or as a witness—a hostile witness, if necessary—what would your answer be under oath to the question: Did you, a CSI, certified by the ICSIA and the state of Colorado, suspect that your UAS units had recorded a fresh murder scene along with the possible perpetrator fleeing that scene today, Tuesday, April 7th, this year, between the hours of nine and ten in the morning, and, if you did so suspect, did you report this suspicion to the appropriate authorities? I'm referring, of course, to Idaho's Failure to Report law, Idaho Code Section 19-4301A."

Jessie felt her face go hot. Her dad saw it. So did the sheriff. She didn't answer. All dogs were on their feet, their focus on Sheriff Reid, and not in a good way.

*

SURROUNDED BY HER CANINE PACK, her copies of the search warrant and a receipt of her property in hand, Jessie watched the two S.O. rigs depart. Oddly, all her property had been handled by the sheriff and put into his unit. He wouldn't allow his captain to help. At least she thought it odd until she read, word by word, the actual warrant and note from the judge that was attached. Then she understood. Her dad's lawyer had come through as promised.

When the sheriff's rigs finally disappeared from sight, her laptop, her four external drives, and two quadcopters with them, her dad blew out a breath. "Jessie, I think you need to tell me *all* of what's going on."

Yeah, she did.

"...And if I need to get you a good defense attorney."

Probably.

***

5 – Assessments

JESSIE'S GRANDDAD WAS NOT in a good mood. He made that clear at breakfast. He considered the confiscation of Jessie's property not just an outrage, but grand larceny. "And, as for you, young lady," he said, jabbing his fork at her, his eyes nailing hers, "you need to stick to working dogs, not those newfangled contraptions that put you in this pickle."

"*No*, Granddad." Jessie rarely would argue with her granddad, but, knowing him well, she wasn't going to let this escalate to one of his ultimatums. Her dad, sitting across from her, ducked his head, his attention moving pointedly to his plate. But his secret smile crept its way to his lips as her granddad exploded.

"What do you mean, 'no'?!" And Jessie swore that, if sparks could ignite from Darby's eyes, they would have. "If you hadn't flown those contraptions, none of this would have happened, and you wouldn't be out thousands upon thousands of dollars."

Jessie saw her gram give her a tiny downward head cue, then a little smile. She got the message. *Go softly.*

He means to protect me. And she took the cue. "I want to do search and rescue, Granddad. And I want to do it the best way possible. That means using drones combined with dogs."

"No, it *doesn't!* Dogs do just fine all by themselves."

It was an old argument. It was a good argument, too. But Jessie wanted better for every life involved—the victims *and* the searchers, including dogs when they were employed. The recent loss of a National Guard helicopter and its crew out searching for lost skiers was a case in point. Drones did it safer and cheaper.

"Finding dead bodies shouldn't wind up with private property confiscated. It's *un-American*, I tell you!" Darby snapped. "Next time, you just fly those bugs onward and ignore something like that that's going to get you in Dutch with the sheriff. Heck, I know Landon Reid and his dad *and* his granddad. I can't believe a Reid would do this to an Idaho citizen."

Jessie didn't remind Darby that Idaho didn't yet consider her a citizen again. She hadn't been living back home long enough to qualify. Nor did she think that Sheriff Reid had any compunction about property seizure.

The department she'd worked for down in Colorado certainly hadn't.

"Anywhoo," her grandfather continued, his voice mollifying. "Enough of all that. I can see plain enough you'll not listen to reason. Today, I need your help teaching John how to be a target for the dogs." He wasn't looking at her, but studiously concentrating on cutting up a sausage link like it was tough steak. It was a sign that he accepted her disagreeing with him. "You up for it?" Now, he raised his eyes, glancing slantwise at her.

"I am," Jessie said. *Padded suit, here we come.* Inside, her heart did a little flip, though. She'd held her own and lived to tell about it. With her granddad! ...Or at least stayed equal. He'd listened. That was proven by her dad giving her a wink and a grin.

*

WITH HAT IN HAND and Captain Barry Olmstead standing next to him, Reid expressed his regrets upon informing the Bigsby family of their child's demise.

The mother—Sharon—sat abruptly, her hand going to her mouth. She didn't scream. She didn't weep. She just sat down on the ratty couch, her head bowing down until Landon could no longer see her face.

Her husband stood at the kitchen door, his body stiff, his face a mask. One of the sons—the oldest—stood just behind him. Both men were silent.

What bothered Reid was that nobody asked how, where, why, when, or by whose hand. They didn't ask anything. "We'll need one of you to come down to the morgue and formally identify the deceased once the body is recovered," Landon said gently. "I'm sorry. I'll send a unit when the time comes."

The father nodded. The son just stared, his eyes stony. The mother didn't move, didn't acknowledge, didn't even moan.

"If you need help with burial expenses, the county's got a fund," Landon added softly.

"I'll see you out, Sheriff," Mr. Bigsby said, stepping forward, then around Barry and him to open the front door. The man stood there silently waiting. The soft bong-bong-bong of a clock chimed the hour—8:00 A.M. Reid and Olmstead took their leave.

"Was that about the weirdest thing you've ever seen?" Barry asked as they got in Reid's unit.

Landon didn't know how to answer that. "I guess ...maybe people handle grief in different ways." Then, "I don't have a lot of experience doing this, so...."

"None of us really do, I think. Well, maybe Martin."

The mention of his undersheriff, presently recovering from his third surgery for a gunshot wound received during an attempted arrest that had started as a domestic dispute and ended in suicide by cop, made Landon's temper start to rear its ugly head. Battening it back into its lockdown, he said, "Yeah. Maybe Martin, as you say." Glancing at the captain, then, he answered the rest: "And, *yeah*, Barry, that is about the weirdest reaction I would *not* have expected from a family just informed that their kid had been murdered. That puts them at the top of my watch list as suspects."

"Family is always suspect," Barry replied.

Yeah. So is the boyfriend and any spurned lovers.

*

"OLD DOGS DO IT BETTER, safer." Darby said to John as he helped the young man get the suit on right. "I'm using one of our steadiest, but this still ain't gonna be no picnic, I'm warning you."

"I'm ready," John said.

Jessie very much doubted that. So, she guessed, did her granddad. Until you experience it, you're never 'ready', and this was John's first time.

A six foot, thirty-year-old athlete who adored dogs, John held his professional dog training KA certificate from the Certification Council for Professional Dog Trainers (CCPDT). He wasn't quite KSA (Knowledge and Skills Assessed) quality, yet, like Jessie, Oli, and Darby, but a KA (Knowledge Assessed) was respectable. More importantly, though, he had the proper empathy and attitude. That made him a promising candidate for becoming a permanent part of their operation. But John had never, ever worked with more than pets. Police, protection, and military working dogs were new to him. Today he'd get his real introduction to the more violent end of things. As a target.

Getting a dog to practice the attack on command without jeopardizing the safety, even life, of the person on whom they're practicing that attack requires that person to, not just be wearing a padded protective suit, but to know what to do to encourage the dog that was just learning. Because John was new to this, Darby was not using a young dog, but had brought out one of the seasoned veterans that was back home in retirement. The sole purpose of today's work with John was training *him*.

"The dog's going to go for an arm or a leg," Jessie told John. "Just go with the momentum as he grabs. Don't fight. That comes later, once you've done this a while."

She demonstrated, Darby sending Lido at her. The big male GSD, an eighty pounder, easily took Jessie to the ground, then held her until the stop command, which he instantly obeyed.

"Remember, hands up high will get them to stop."

Darby sent the dog again, and, as he approached at a dead run, Jessie held her hands up in surrender.

The dog stopped and crouched, ready to spring, eyes on her for any aggressive movement. She started to turn her back and the dog crept forward and around, keeping his eyes on hers. She feinted left, and he attacked, taking her down. She went still, and, though growling at her, teeth locked on her arm, he didn't continue to work her. Darby recalled him.

"Okay to try it, John?" she asked once the dog had returned to Darby's side.

"Easy," John said with a grin, but Jessie wasn't so sure he knew what he was about to experience, which proved out moments later as Darby again sent Lido, this time at John.

The young man went down hard, all six foot of him. He freaked out, squirming, fighting, and screaming, which, of course, made the German Shepherd even more ferociously determined. Darby called the stop, and Jessie went over to help John up. "The more you fight and struggle, the more they're going to work you until you give up."

"That was *terrifying!*"

"It is. They're powerful and quick."

The young man looked dubious. "I'm not sure I can do this without reacting."

"Well, you don't have to do it. We can call it off."

He straightened up, and all but braced himself. "Yes, I do. You did it. You *do* it. I've seen you. I'd like to try, again."

"Okay. We'll do it together. Now, take a deep breath and relax. And try not to fight it. Think of it as a game. Play dead once he gets a hold of you. Give up. Let him know he's won."

"Some game," John muttered, but he put his head protection back on. Then, looking toward Darby, gave the ready signal.

Darby sent the dog.

***

"*Aus, AUS!*" her granddad bellowed, but the dog was now in a frenzy.

Darby ran up, John approaching, too, but Jessie, feeling almost ethereally calm inside, warned them off. "You'll get bitten. Let me handle it." And, all the while, the young dog tore at her suit, trying to find flesh. This was getting dangerous.

Jessie started making long, particular vocalizations, her body as still and limp as possible, and, finally the dog eased up. "*Guter Hund, braver Hund. Ganz ruhig,*" Jessie whispered. And, finally, something registered. The young dog stopped and just stood panting hard, watching her, eyes bloodshot. He was very stressed.

Darby and John crept in from either side, John with the pole, its catch loop open. John got the loop on, and then Darby went in and snapped on a lead, reinforcing '*aus*' and asking the dog to '*fuss*'. Still confused, the dog again downed instead, then gave Darby his head, closed his eyes for a moment, yawned and whined. Darby took John's catch loop off, gave the young Malinois strokes and squatted down by him, encouraging and calming him with praise.

"How old is he, Granddad?" Jessie asked when it was safe to get up.

"A little over six months. First time working a live person instead of a bite pad. But he's had all the pre-training. He's impeccable …usually, anyway. Perfect in fact. You name it, he does it right."

Checking her suit, she reset some of the straps, tightening them. "He's big for six months. Forty pounds or so?"

Her grandfather nodded. "Forty-six this morning."

"Which line is he?"

"Cabil."

All straps secured, Jessie gave him the thumbs up. "Let's try again."

John, who was white in the face, shook his head. "Unbelievable," he commented, and walked back to the side.

Even Darby looked skeptical. His color was up. "You up for it? He worked you pretty bad. Scared me, even, Jessica."

"Hm-mmm. I'm fine. Send him."

And this time, the dog did better. By the fifth send, he'd figured it out. "Smart boy," Jessie said to Darby.

"That's a *big* relief," he said. Then: "Couldn't do it without you, Jessica Marie." Her granddad turned to pointedly look at her. "What'd you do to get him to quit his attack when he went nuts that first time?"

She grinned. "Dog whispering."

He groaned and shook his head. "Right."

"Are we done?"

"Yep. ...Thought we were done and he was done *for* forty-five minutes ago."

"I've got a test set up for my HRD dogs, so if you don't need me—"

"Go to it, but where's the test, so we don't go messing it up when we take the youngsters out for group training?"

"I set up on the eighty just south of the big cedar and larch stand on the west section."

"The hay field near Dr. Lorenson's?"

"Yes."

"That's a hike, but okay. We'll keep the pups clear of your test."

"Thanks, Granddad."

*

"YOU REALLY THINK the Bigsbys are smart enough to do something to somebody and leave no real evidence?" Barry asked as they backed out of the drive.

Landon cocked an eye at his captain. He thought about the question and didn't answer until they pulled up to the light. "Don't know."

"Neither do I, but, honestly, I don't think so. They're not particularly the clean and tidy types, if you get my drift."

Barry was right, of course. You had to be meticulous and knowledgeable to be able to avoid leaving traces of your presence, and the Bigsbys weren't either one. Their house and yard was unkempt, and the only reading it seemed like they did, if even that, which Landon sincerely doubted, was the Good Book, a fancy copy of which had lain like a badge on their coffee table. "Wonder how we're doing on Sue's apartment. Want to head over with me?"

"Sure," Barry answered, and Landon turned toward the lake.

When they got to Sue Bigsby's apartment, the landlord was standing there, his face shocked. No, he hadn't seen either Sue or her roommate, one Debbie Ferris, not since he'd had to replace the hot water heater a couple of months back. Yes, they always paid their rent on time. Yes, they were good tenants. Sue worked as a waitress, and Debbie worked as a maid in a local motel. That's all he knew.

Landon wondered how the kids, both twenty-year-olds by DMV records, could afford to rent what amounted to a luxury view apartment on less than minimum wage jobs. Pooling resources, they still couldn't have afforded it on what they made, even with great tips.

The hint of an answer came in the form of a lockbox filled with fist-sized rolls of twenty, fifty, and hundred dollar bills. "There must be over ten grand here," Deputy Keith Winters said, his gloved hands holding open the bag containing them for another deputy to snap an evidentiary photo.

They found no drugs, the most obvious potential income source. Nor did they find any evidence of prostitution. There was nothing incriminating on the girls' phones or laptops, either.

They did find scribbled-on napkins from one of the two local party bars that held weekend raves—poetry. "Have somebody check out those bars, Barry," Reid growled. "See if anybody knows anything."

"Will do."

"And I want a BOLO for Debbie Ferris. *Find* her. Preferably alive."

***

7 – High Praise

JESSIE HAD TO FOCUS. But focus was evading her. Her lack of it distracted Milo and Mitch. Instead of working the ground, they kept looking in her direction, emitting soft, high-pitched, questioning whines. They were worried, not for themselves, but for her.

Finally, she sat down on the ground, called them over, and, as they settled in beside her, one to either side, she draped her arms on both. "Sorry, guys. I'm just totally adrift, now. The whole plan is just a hazy mess. I can't see a good, safe way forward without the drones."

Milo sat up, raised a paw and landed it on her crossed leg, then reached his nose down and gave her a dog kiss. Mitch wriggled, scooted, boosting himself with his front paws until he managed to lay his whole head on her lap, then twisted himself till he was tummy up, legs in the air. She laughed—her dogs, her joy.

Taking a breath, she pushed Mitch off and got up. "Let's try it again, shall we? And, this time, I promise, I'll concentrate so you can, too."

The dogs both stood, their eyes on her. She gave her 'all', 'human', and 'dead' signals, then, signing 'search', said, "Okay. *Such.* Seek. Find it."

Both dogs trotted forward and, as she'd taught them, began quartering the search field, each taking a part of it, noses to the ground.

In moments, Milo alerted, laying down into his characteristic sphinx crouch-down. Mitch was still sweeping back and forth in a series of figure eights. Then he too alerted, stopping dead in his tracks, downing, his eyes focused on the ground.

"*Fein! Brave Hunde,*" Jessie called. "Good dogs!" she repeated, running up to drop a weighted evidence marker on the ground where they each indicated—knew they were accurate to where and what she'd buried there yesterday—and grinned.

Turning to them, again, she said, "*Such.* Seek. Find it," and, again, the dogs began quartering the field.

Within twenty minutes, Milo had alerted to eight different spots where she'd buried artificial, or, more properly, synthetic human remains, Mitch to seven. Milo had nailed all of his, Mitch all but one of his. Neither dog had alerted to the pieces of dead animals she'd buried in the search field—dead mice brought in by one or another of their cats as 'offerings' which Jessie collected and froze until she needed them.

Walking out to the one Mitch had missed, she asked him to 'find it', and, after a good five minutes, when he just couldn't seem to, she stepped up, pointed to the spot and called to him. "Is it here?" she asked. He came up, sniffed repeatedly, wagged his tail, then sat down, his eyes on her.

Jessie frowned. Why wasn't he picking up on it?

Trotting over to her bag, she pulled out a trowel and went back to the spot. Digging down, she hit pay dirt and saw the problem—her error. In her fog of misery, she'd put the scent rag in the ground, but still inside its sealed bag. Of course he couldn't smell it. "I'm so, so sorry, Mitch. My bad," she said, bending down to give him a nose kiss.

He wagged and poked his nose between her knees, then bounded up to lick her chin. She was forgiven.

Walking back over to her starting spot, she called them to her, then asked them to pay attention. Pulling out a sealed bag from her pocket, she opened it and let both dogs take a sniff. Then, she asked them to sniff again. When they both had, she put it away, then used her sign for 'one specific', 'human', and 'dead' before again calling for the search.

Jessie was asking them to discriminate between all of the different dead remains she had buried and pick only the two spots that were identical scents to the scent in the bag.

Within a few minutes, both Mitch and Milo downed, and Jessie could have wept. Both of them nailed it. "*Gute Hunde, ganz brave Hunde. Wundervoll!*"

She ran out to them, hugging them, rubbing them, and, of course, offering their "mostest, favoritist" treat for her heartfelt thank you. "Such good dogs, such wonderful dogs, such *great* dogs," she crooned, laughing with them as they jumped and bounded around in 'happy dog' joy, Milo's bounces putting him up at eye level with her, Mitch's almost that. They knew.

Jessie just wanted to shout it out to the world, but, of course, the world wasn't watching. Just her. She had learned to successfully communicate with Mitch and Milo, and they had, in turn, learned her 'rudimentary dog-speak-done-human-style'.

"I'm going to assume that something really good happened," came her granddad's call.

Startled, Jessie looked to the far side of the field, over near where the woods started. Milo and Mitch both instantly sat, their heads swiveling to stare at their audience. There, emerging from the woods on their horses with a pack of eight dogs around them were her dad and her granddad.

She grinned. They'd been spying on her. "They just aced, not only human remains detection, but then scent discrimination to choose only one specific dead human's remains," Jessie called.

"Can we come out there?"

Jessie nodded. "Yes."

Maneuvering around the tiny markers, both her dad's and her granddad's horses ambled up. Her dad dismounted and dropped his horse's reins. At her granddad's signal, every one of their dogs immediately sat.

Her dad walked up to her, reached out and hugged her. "Watching you work," he said, then shook his head. "Jessie, that was amazing. You're actually communicating with them. It's uncanny."

"Thanks, Dad."

"Our own Dr. Doolittle," her granddad said with a grin. "Solid gold work, Jessica Marie."

And that, coming from her granddad, was high praise, indeed.

***

8 – Clubbing

AN APPOINTMENT HAD BEEN SET UP to interview one Bill Craven, owner of The Craven Inn, and Landon decided he'd go along with his lieutenant to meet the owner of the town's most notorious liquor joint and dance club. Thirty-one-year-old Bill Craven had a reputation, and it wasn't a good one. Landon's plan was to let his lieutenant do the talking. He just wanted to study the man as he answered. Their appointment was at four. The place opened for business at five.

"Yeah, I know the girls," Bill said when he finally sauntered out of his back room ten minutes late. His wavy, dark hair all mussed and uncombed said he'd just gotten out of bed. So did the pillow marks on his grinning face.

He didn't invite them to sit. He didn't offer them anything to drink. Just stood smirking, his hands stuffed in the waistband of some garishly colored pants that looked like he was actually still wearing his pajamas—adult-sized kids pajamas. "Used to come here every weekend. They'd show off on the poles." The man gestured with his head, his hands never leaving his waistband. "Haven't seen them for a couple of weeks, now."

Landon's eyes flicked to the two dance poles up on either side of the raised platform, between which sat a counter that held lots of electronics.

"They were pretty entertaining. Made a good bit, I think, on tips."

Landon frowned at that. So was that where the money had come from? Or did Craven have back rooms for entrepreneurial prostitution? He blew a breath, and saw Bill Craven notice.

"Nope," the man said, as if reading his mind. "Make my money on booze and cover charges."

"How much does it cost to get in?" Red asked.

"For you? Nothing."

"For the patrons," Landon said dryly.

"Twenty bucks on Monday, Tuesday, and Thursday. Thirty on Wednesday, and fifty bucks on Friday and Saturday nights. Plus I.D, of course. Always I.D." He smirked even more as he said it.

Fifty bucks!

"We do a 'girls night free' and a 'stag night', too. Once a month each. On Tuesday or Thursday."

Yeah. Those are the nights when the P.D. calls us to help break up the fights and help take kids to the ER.

"How many people are in here on any given week night and how many on Friday and Saturday night?" Red asked.

"Monday, Tuesday, and Thursday, maybe ten to twenty, except on the free nights. It loads up, then. Wednesday is over the hump night, so it gets up to thirty or forty total. Weekends, we're up to fifty on the floor during peak hours and, sometimes, we'll hit capacity—eighty—if we can get this one DJ in."

"And Sue and Debbie came in on weekends?"

"Yeah. Sometimes Wednesdays, too, but that was hit or miss. They made the most booty for their booty show on the weekends."

So maybe that is *how they made their wad*, Landon thought.

"Did they always come in together?"

"Yeah. Never seen 'em apart, actually. Always left together, too."

"And anyone in particular that hung out with Sue or Debbi?" Red asked.

"Just the usual lesbos."

"Lesbos?" Red came back, scorn saturating his voice.

"Yeah," and, again Bill Craven's eyes flicked to Landon's. "Girls who are into other girls. Big hit with the guys, too. They somehow think two or three gals rubbing themselves against each other is a turn on. To each his own, and all that."

"And which guys paid the most attention?" Landon asked.

The man shook his head, but his eyes slid sideways—lying. "Couldn't tell you that. Don't know the younger crowd much, and that's who comes here. They all kinda look the same, y'know? Especially under the lights."

"But you know Sue and Debbie."

Craven laughed. "Everybody knows Sue and Debbie."

"Why?"

"Because they flaunt it more than anybody else."

"You have surveillance tape?" Landon asked.

"Erased every morning unless there's a robbery or assault."

"Right." *And probably erased then, too, unless it's somebody robbing you.*

"Have you kept any from the last month?"

"Nope. Sorry. It's programmed to auto erase unless I take a copy of it before 4AM."

"All bases covered, huh?" Landon remarked.

"Got to. Get folks coming in here wanting to know if their kid or their wife or their husband was here. I can't go squealing on my customers and all, y'know. They'd stop coming, and I'd be out my livelihood."

"Right."

Outside, Red stood looking down the street to the other dance club. "Want to check them out, too?"

"We can. Do we need an appointment for this one?"

"Nah. I know Jerry Bingham. Besides, they're open from two in the afternoon till two at night. Serve some pretty good food, too, if you're hungry."

"No."

They walked the block, but quizzing the owner there netted them nothing useful. This joint was a "cowboy" club that played live music—country western, with mostly local groups doing covers, the patrons invited to come up and sing if they wanted. It served all age groups with some nights—the slow ones—reserved for old timers. "We even feature some square dancing. Offer classes, too. Got a good caller. Local fellow."

Pete Campbell, the manager, said he'd never seen either girl, and, yes, they did keep their video surveillance for a week. Then it got overwritten. "Women who come here are …looking to catch them a man. Guys who come here are looking to catch them a lay. We've got a dress code, too. No bling, no pasties—gotta be wearing a top and a bottom—but, yes, booty shorts allowed, though few wear them. Must wear hat and boots, though," Pete told them. "We're strict about the hat and boots. Gotta look the part." He grinned saying it.

And that left out Sue and Debbie. Their wardrobes had held no boots, just mostly spike heels and flats. There certainly hadn't been any Stetsons®, Resistols®, or even kids' cowboy hats from Walmart® in their possession.

"Well, that was pretty much a wash," Red said as they headed back to the unit.

"Lesbians," Landon said, thinking.

"What about 'em?"

"Fake or real for Sue and Debbie?"

Red shrugged. "I think it's mostly a fad—a gimmick to be 'different'. I think most people 'grow out of it', if you follow."

"I follow. But were they just mining for money, playing at it, or were they actually gay?"

Red shrugged, again. "Could be all three between the two of them, I suppose."

"Sue's pink hair that she was so well known for, that tells me she was just playing it for the money, I think."

"I don't know. She started dying it that way before she graduated high school. Got her kicked out of her house."

"And you know this how?"

"It's in her records. She got picked up that night by the P.D.. They took her to the women's shelter since she was already eighteen going on nineteen."

"Ah. Guess I should have read a little deeper in the file."

"Naw. That's what you've got us for," Red said with a grin. "And, actually, I'm finding myself kind of invested in this case. I don't like the smell of it."

"I don't either," Landon admitted.

"I know. You wouldn't have called Wilber in otherwise, and I'm glad you did. I think this is serious."

"Me, too. You heard anything?"

"Nope. He's still huddled up with the ME, last I heard."

"Taking that long, huh?"

"Seems so."

And that did not bode well.

***

9 – A Local Killer

IT WAS JUST LIGHT ENOUGH to see, the morning twilight still not bright enough to 'see color'. Jessie was just starting her morning run, the dogs trotting along with her, stopping here and there to sniff something delicious to their senses as Jessie ran on.

Acer suddenly bounded to her side. Then the rest came running, dodged in front of her, then stopped, barring her way, their heads up, ears pricked. Forced to stop, Jessie wondered if a bear was nearby, hoping it wasn't a grizzly. One had been sighted in the area last week. She checked her right pocket for the bear bomb, then pulled the canister of bear spray out of her left and waited.

Long seconds later, faintly she heard the sound of a vehicle. That vehicle got closer, then faded again. *It's on the old Forest Service road.* It was an odd thing to hear this early. The public had the right to be there, but, earlier than a half an hour before sunrise, it was unusual.

The body and the red truck her drones had sighted flashed to mind. Certainly, the killer wouldn't come back up, would he? *Could be a turkey hunter getting an early start.* That was the only season open at the moment. *Could be a poacher, too.*

The sound of the vehicle returned and faded twice more as it climbed, then faded completely. The dogs relaxed, and Jessie resumed her run. But her nerves were on edge, especially when the dogs moved to position themselves strategically around her, Acer and Britta to either side of her, Milo and Mitch in front, Queenie, Sumi, and Oso bringing up the rear.

Jessie hadn't taught them that. They'd come to that arrangement on their own. *We really are a pack*, Jessie thought. What bothered her was that they considered her the most vulnerable of their number. She was 'the pup to be protected'.

Thinking about it, though, maybe she was. She didn't carry more than bear repellent, despite both her dad's and granddad's admonishments that she needed to, at least, take a revolver with her. "Just in case."

In case of what? Anything smaller than a .357 magnum couldn't stop a grizzly, a black bear, or a charging moose. Bear spray and bombs were better, and she had those tucked in her pocket, more in the small emergency pack on her back. A gun was good against people, feral dogs, scaring off a big cat or the occasional wolverine—that sort of thing—but mostly against people, and there just weren't that many people to be wary of in their locale. The incident two days ago was an anomaly. Still, though, maybe she should pack iron—her .22, maybe—just in case. *Tomorrow,* she told herself. She'd do it starting tomorrow.

*

LANDON'S PHONE BUZZED as he was just getting a mug out of the cupboard. He ignored it. It was too early for phone calls—just after 5AM—and he needed coffee before talking to anyone.

Moments later, the darned thing buzzed, again, though. This time, he glanced at it, recognized the number, and answered, "Sheriff Reid." In the background, he heard the distinct sound of a small plane's engine. Schmidt was already headed home.

"This is Captain Wilber Schmidt, CSI, Idaho State Police, Sheriff Reid. Can you hear me all right?'

"Loud and clear, Captain."

"I've finished my report and left it in your office. Evidence is logged in, samples, including semen samples, sent off to the lab. I'll have my office bill yours, but I wanted you to know that I think you may have a serial killer on your hands. He may be early to mid stages, but definitely showing all the hallmarks of having orchestrated this before. This is just my opinion, but this young woman is not your victim zero."

Reid's stomach had lurched at the word 'orchestrated'. Now it did a full flip. "What makes you say that, Captain?"

"It's all in my report, but, well, like the lack of hesitation marks on the body. Your ME and I are in complete agreement about this. There's also the distinct and careful lack of evidence all around the scene—no misplaced footprints, no fibers or hairs, not even tire tracks that were distinct and recoverable. He made sure to park on rock. On purpose. Like I said, I think he's done this before. Why he wasn't careful about the evidence left on the body makes me suspicious that what you actually have is a leader and an apprentice-helper, the apprentice being the rapist and someone the principal considers disposable. I'm guessing it's the helper's DNA we'll have recovered from the victim's body."

Now, he was wide awake. Without coffee. And he wouldn't need any. "All right, Captain. And thank you."

"One more thing, Sheriff."

"Go ahead."

"I think your perp knows the area."

Reid frowned. "A local, then?"

"I'd say so. I'd check out other locations in your county with similar terrain. That he chose that particular spot says something. Again, it's all in my report. In detail."

"All right. Thank you for telling me."

"Till next time." The man paused, then added, "Because there will be a next time."

A chill ran down Reid's neck. He felt the start of a headache and his stomach had turned into a festering black pit. *Not if I can help it.*

Homicides were rare in his county—maybe two or three in a year. Most of them were heat-of-the-moment shootings at a bar or between antagonistic neighbors. Then, there was the occasional domestic like the one that had almost killed his undersheriff—Landon hated those.

Once in a blue moon, there might be a death as a result of a home or property invasion, but it was usually the perp who got shot—Darwin Awards®. Mostly, his county was quiet and well-behaved. Farmers, ranchers, and small business owners didn't have the time or the inclination to act out, and Landon liked it that way. It was those they employed who mostly got into trouble, but that trouble usually involved money …or the lack of it.

Reid, like his dad before him, tried to *keep* their county that way—quiet. While his dad had done it with a swift, uncompromising response, Reid did it mostly by trying to stay ahead of trouble …or at least even with it, using special intercession workers provided by the local women's shelter, NAMI, and Health and Human Services, his reservists going along to keep things peaceable. It had taken him all last year to organize, but it was proving out, keeping trouble at a minimum. Of course, there were the teenagers who could get a bit wild. But, mostly, a couple of swift kicks in the right direction got them straightened out fast. And, since he'd been one himself here, he knew all the places used for keggers and other illicit activities.

Still, though, when all was tallied, he didn't have much practice at any of it. But he was duly elected, the youngest sheriff on record in Idaho, and there it was. And all because he was a Reid, and folks in this county trusted the Reids because of his dad's and his granddad's reputations, both sheriffs of this county before they'd retired to pass it on to their sons.

'Head them off at the pass and shoot to kill. Saves the taxpayers a load of money', his dad still always told him. Repeatedly. Landon tried not to follow the shoot to kill advice, but he certainly did the rest. This time, though, there'd been no advanced warning of trouble brewing. This time, somebody had beat him to, then through, the pass. They were way ahead of him.

***

"I'll do it when I come to let the horses out. I'm heading to do the chickens, then over to the horse barn, now."

"You mind that you don't go getting nailed by that rooster."

"Yeah, I'm good. He's a pushover …when you're armed with a garbage can lid."

Darby chuckled. "That'll do it. Just so you know, your dad, your grandmother, and me have to meet somebody in town this afternoon. John will be here, of course."

"Okay," Jessie answered.

"Give my mare an extra ration, would you?" he called after her. "She's getting a little weedy-looking."

"Okay."

In the chicken yard, the rooster ignored her. The momma duck and her mate, on the other hand, took swipes at her. Jessie ignored the birds and finished gathering the eggs, then loaded the feeders. She got a pinch on the back of her calf as she scraped the floor clean.

Turning on the creatures, she shooed them off.

The ducks hissed at her.

"Okay, okay. Nobody's going to touch your ducklings, Sadie Duck and Sam. Back it on off."

The ducks both reared up, wings flapping.

When they settled, Jessie took advantage and swooped Sam up. The drake immediately hollered until Jessie gave him strokes and a kiss on the beak. Calm again, she gave him a few more strokes, and the bird rewarded her by tucking his bill into the crook of her arm.

"There, now. Back to your family." She put the drake down, and, uttering soft mutterings, he waddled back to his mate who was now playing in the kiddie pool with her ducklings, scooping ground grain out of the feeder, wetting it, then feeding it to them, one by one, before wetting her own bill-full and swallowing it down.

The rooster decided it was his turn, but a glare his way got him backed off, again, especially when she picked up the garbage can lid she'd leaned against the coop wall. With a fluffing ruffle of feathers, he turned tail and stalked off.

Done, she opened the door to the chicken yard for them so they could free range, then headed to the horse barn.

Chesterton, her old gelding, nickered his welcome when she came in. "Hungry, old man?" she asked.

The other horses came in from their runs. As usual, Snake, her new horse, started pounding the floor boards of her stall. "Quit that, Snake," she snapped with her best 'hard' voice, but, of course, Snake already knew it was all bluff. The four-year-old mare already had figured out that nobody was going to 'make' her.

Jessie rolled her eyes. "Brat!"

Tossing in flakes of hay to each, she gave special strokes to Chesterton before she got the fork and wheel barrow and started in on morning cleaning. The four geldings' stalls were, as usual, the easy, quick jobs. All of them pretty much pooped in one place, peed in another, and kept their feet out of those spots. She was done in moments, the horses shifting this way and that as she fluffed their bedding back into shape. The three mare's stalls were typically a mess, especially Snake's. Jessie got the apple picker and started the job of sifting through the straw-shavings mix. "You know, if you'd try a little, you'd get your goodies faster," she told the wily creature.

As if in answer, the mare reached a nose over and gave her a playful push. Jessie grinned and rewarded her with a scratch to her favorite spot just below and beside her withers. "There ya go, Snake."

Tess and Sassy's stalls needed bedding added, so Jessie had to fire up the Bobcat and go get a bucketful. By the time she was done, her dad walked in. "We've got all the kennels cleaned," he said.

"That was fast."

"Those new floors make it a lot easier."

Jessie nodded his way. "Worth the expense, then?"

"Definitely. I'll do the grain."

"Tess needs an extra ration, Granddad says."

"He told me, though she looks fat enough to me."

Jessie agreed, but they'd feed her up, anyway. Darby knew horses better than either of them.

By the time she was done shoveling in the sawdust and getting it leveled, Oli was leaning against the wall, waiting with the last two cans of feed. "Hop to it, Jessie, my Jessie. It's closing on breakfast time."

She grinned. "Yeah, and you do love your oatmeal."

His face went still. His nose crinkled a little. "Oatmeal this morning?"

She laughed out loud. "No. It's something better. Gram and I got it ready last night. I put it in to bake when I got back from my run."

"Breakfast casserole!" he guessed, and she nodded. "Come on, then. Time's a-wastin'. Race you to the house."

Of course he beat her with his longer legs. "I should get a handicap to compensate for your height," she complained.

"And I should get twice the handicap for being a quarter century older than you."

He had a point.

***

11 – The Perp

REID TOOK A BITE of an already cold sausage and egg muffin, chewing the tasteless, rubbery thing as he sifted through email, dumping what he could and marking the ones in order of priority that he'd need to answer. Next, he pulled up both Wilber's and the ME's report, attached them to a group email, and hit send to distribute them to his deputies. Then, checking the collate box, he printed out sixteen full sets of the grisly things for the reservists he'd called in: Cause of death, strangulation. But, worse, was the violence discovered upon turning the body over. Not only had the victim been raped—violently—but the body had been mutilated. The very thought made Landon's stomach churn. The pictures made his eyes hurt. The only blessing was that the mutilation had been done post mortem. *Thank God for some mercies.* A plus was that they had the perp's DNA, now, but it would take weeks to get that information back.

"Boss? We're ready."

Landon stood and, rubbing away the images that seemed imprinted in his eyes, went to the ready room where everyone who should be there *was* there. Murder, especially something this bad, made everybody sit up and take notice.

He passed out copies of the reports among the reservists—paid reservists. He'd managed that with some wrangling. Nobody paid reservists …but his county did. Now. Only fair. Even half pay was better than nothing. "Okay, Red's briefed you, I know, but we've got some video of who we think is the perp leaving the scene right after dumping the body that I want you all to see. …John, if you'd get the lights? Red, go ahead and put the evidence on the screen."

As the pertinent parts of the audio-video data began to play, Landon felt the mood of the room shift from normal to one of frustration and despair at the sight of the body from something like a couple of hundred feet up to down in close. When the second feed started, though, the room's atmosphere shifted again to something he couldn't quite put his finger on—maybe hope mixed with anger?—at the appearance of the red pickup truck with its driver just visible, if a blur, emerging from the cover of forest onto the old dirt road that was cut into the mountain. The image blurred then stilled again, closing in, and they got a good look at the driver, but his or her face was contorted and blurred. Later, the recording swooped in to get the front, then the back of the truck—no license plates.

Everyone sat forward. Somebody said, "He's wearing a mask of some sort. Like a nylon stocking or something."

Then, a voice Landon recognized as reservist Sam Hull asked, "These come from satellite?"

"Drones. One Jessica Marie Anderson was flying her new drones and caught this."

"The search dog girl?"—Reservist Sam Hull, again.

And that was the second time someone associated Miss Anderson with dogs. "That's her dad," Landon answered, trying to keep the irritation he felt out of his voice.

"Nope. He and his dad train MWDs." Then, at Landon's look, Sam said, "Military working dogs. And, actually, military, police, protection, and bomb dogs, not SAR …search and rescue dogs. Jessie does SAR."

"And you know this how?" Landon asked dryly.

Sam, who was a couple of years north of seventy, but tougher than wang leather and still outfoxing their self-defense trainer, smirked. "I'm good friends with Darby, her granddad. He dotes on the girl. That's a secret, though. Don't tell nobody. A lot of sparks between them about canines."

Sam's slipping into that specific 'good ol' boy' redneck jargon on the 'don't tell nobody' along with his pronunciation of the last—KA-AAY-nines—said it all—Darby Anderson was in good standing with those who counted as 'good folk' in this country. Landon sighed, but quashed his urge to shake his head.

"Can we go back to the first one?" This question was from one of the S.O.'s newest hires, David Kins, hired by Landon's dad just before he retired. The kid had, at the time of his hiring, been just barely old enough to make the force, but he was proving to be a good deputy. "Sure," Landon answered, glad for the rescue. "Red, do the honors, would you?" and the recording started again.

"Stop!" the kid yelped. "Go back a couple of seconds." Then, "Is that the perp? That shadow?"

Landon frowned, walked up to the wall screen and squinted. "Where?"

The kid stood and approached the screen. His finger circled. "Right here."

Again, Landon squinted. Then, instead, he stepped back and tried to see if distance helped so he could see what the kid was seeing. He failed. "Red, run it back five seconds, then run it in slow mo, would you?"

Despite that, Landon still couldn't make out what Kins was seeing.

"Can I try my hand on that laptop?" Dave asked. "I'm pretty good at manipulating video to enhance it."

"Oka-ay," Landon said. "Use a copy, not the originals, though."

A few minutes later, the kid nodded. "Ready." He touched something and what had been small was now focused and large. "…Right …*here*!"

Soft bursts of exclamations erupted through the room. Landon shook his head in amazement. The image, taken while the drone was first arriving showed a human figure just disappearing into the woods. "Good job, Dave!" He turned to the room. "And there's the back of who might very well be our perp!"

"By my figures, he's got to be somewhere around six feet," Dave said.

Startled, Landon asked how he knew that. "By the size of the victim who's five-foot-six, according to the ME's report. Taking in the time of day and the angle of his shadow, I'm guessing, though. Somebody good at this could probably give you an exact height, maybe even a weight, but, hey, at least we know it's probably a male—slim hips and no boobs—he's thin, and he's got short, dark, wavy hair, right?"

...Which narrowed it down to a few thousand possibilities in this county alone, never mind people from outside the area. Same with what they now could identify as probably a 2007 to 2013 red, long bed Chevy pickup—probably a 1500, and, for sure, a single cab. It wasn't much, but at least it was something.

Landon turned to the room. "Okay, people. You know the drill. I want to know everything there is to know about Sue Bigsby, and I want Debbie Ferris found. We need to know where that money came from, too, and we really need to find that truck. Start with DMV records on the truck and go from there. Check out every red truck that matches in this county, and, if that doesn't hit pay dirt, move out from there."

Turning to Kins, he said, "Dave? My office."

The kid's face blanched. "Y-Yes, sir."

Landon sighed. *Why do they always think I'm going to eat them?!*

***

12 – Dead Wrong

"SO, HOW DO YOU KNOW so much about enhancing video and figuring out height and the like?" Landon asked.

Visibly, Dave relaxed. "It's a hobby."

"A hobby." *Some hobby*. Maybe this kid should have gone to college, not the police academy.

"Yes, sir."

"You know anything about anything else that might help us?"

The young man's face dropped to look at his hands. "Not really. I do fly drones, though—cheap ones—so I'm used to looking at their feeds."

"You *do*," Landon said dryly and shook his head. "And never mind the privacy laws!"

The kid squirmed. "I only fly them in remote areas. ...Sorry, sir."

Landon indicated the two sitting parked on his counter and reminded himself that he needed to lock them up, since, thanks to obvious interference by someone, he and his office were personally responsible for them …for all of Ms. Anderson's equipment. The terseness of the note from Judge Peterson had been clear. "And what do you think of those drones?"

Dave's face lit up. "Oh, man. Those are *state*-of-the-*art!* They're way beyond anything I've ever even seen except in videos!"

"So they're good ones?"

"Oh, *yeah!*"

"Is there any way of proving that those drones took those audio-visual recordings?"

The kid looked startled. "Yeah. The metadata is still intact on the videos and each drone has its own signature." The kid paused. "Well, unless somebody messed with them."

"Can you tell?"

Dave grinned. "That's easy. We download the flight record and GPS data from their onboard chips—kinda like an airplane's black box."

"Oka-aay. Can you do that for me without disturbing the evidence?"

"Sure. Just need a thumb drive."

Landon frowned and, opening his drawer, extracted the thumb drive Jessie had handed him. "Would that be on this?"

"What's on it?"

"I don't know. The woman who owns those drones gave it to me."

"God, I'd *love* to meet her!"

Landon stared. The kid practically had a mental hard-on. "Let's stick to this, for the moment, shall we?"

"Yes, sir. Sorry, sir."

The kid got up. "If I can use your computer, sir, I can tell you if what you need is on that stick to prove what we have to," Dave said.

Landon stood up. "Be my guest."

Moments later, the kid accessed the data on the tiny data storage device Ms. Anderson had given him and, that quick, Dave Kins showed Reid that, not only had the woman provided the entire video feeds of both machines, but also the downloads of their entire flight history, including the ones that matched the IDs of their evidence.

"Ooo. There's something else on here, too," Dave said, excitement in his voice. "Look! She enhanced it! And it's an *expert* job!"

And it was. Their perp was loud and clear. But the face was still all a blur.

"Can you tell if that blur was done by the owner of the drones?"

The kid went back and got the laptop from the other room, then checked things Landon couldn't even begin to recognize. "No. It's all virgin footage," Kins said.

"Then what's blurred his face?"

"A stocking maybe? Or a mask of some kind?"

Landon shook his head. Something, for sure. Still, though, they now had enough detail to I.D. the truck. Landon could see practically every dent and every scratch on its front, back, top, hood, and bed, and even a few on the driver's side door. "Get detail stills from that footage printed and out to the troops," he told Kins.

"Yes, sir."

Watching the enhancement through one more time, Reid frowned. Jessica Marie Anderson was, it seemed, pretty good at her job. "Ex-job," he muttered. Now he wanted to know why she no longer worked that job. What had she done to get her pressured to resign, because that was his bet about what had actually happened. PTSD? No way. What had she done?

His eyes went to the drones. She had not been happy with him. Well, he wasn't happy with her, either. She'd known that was a murder, and she'd not divulged that knowledge. The crime scene had been compromised, evidence lost, all because they'd been investigating what they thought was an injury/accident. But this was murder, and Jessica Anderson had known it right from the start and not said a thing. Landon shook his head, muttering unpleasantries.

Bringing up the 9-1-1 recording, Landon listened to it yet again. There it was. The hesitation, the pauses, the omissions, but, especially, the carefully chosen words. "Smarty." And all because she didn't want to part with her precious equipment was his bet.

On a whim, he dialed Blaine S.O, and, finally, after a run-around, got a call back from the undersheriff, a Reggie Dennison.

"Jessie was really good at her job," the man told him. "She never jumped to conclusions, was meticulous in cataloguing the evidence, and, when you asked the right questions, had brilliant insights into what may have gone down. She pays attention to details. But she does have an aversion to violence and to carrying a gun. That was known from the start before we even hired her. I think it's why she quit the force."

Quit? So she'd really quit? "Elaborate?"

"The gang retaliation we had last fall. We lost a couple of good officers because of that mess, and Jessie was one of them. Right in the middle of an investigation on some beheadings. Our special crime analysis team got stranded in the middle of it, and the S.W.A.T. team couldn't reach us. Destroyed our units. A couple of us took rounds. Between the injured and dead, it was a massacre—a mob against a handful of us. But Jessie's a crack shot, and she's ice under fire. I found that out the hard way. She's the reason she, Jacobs, and I are all still breathing. But the fact that several of our deputies were killed and the fact that both she and her dog were injured—"

"Dog?"

"Yeah. Acer, she called him. Don't know if she still has him or not. He was hurt. Don't know how badly.

Anyway, I think the whole incident destroyed her confidence. I think she blames herself for the deaths. But, under fire, she's got her father's steel. I can personally attest to that, and so can Captain Jacobs. If you need a very good deputy and a great CSI, you can't go wrong with Jessie."

When the man hung up, Landon Reid sat back and thought. He'd been wrong—dead wrong.

***

13 – Surprise Visitor

JESSIE HEARD THE DOGS in her father's kennel complex explode with 'intruder alert'. All her dogs stood up. An all but silent growl rumbled in Milo's throat. Closing out her spreadsheet, Jessie switched screens to those of the security monitors.

It was a sheriff's rig and a dark shadow went through her at the sight of the tall, lanky form of the sheriff getting out of the vehicle. Absently, her hand reached down. Several noses touched it. "*Brave Hunde.* What do you suppose he wants, now? My desktop computer, too?"

The dogs suddenly all sat. Milo then sank into his sphinx crouch. Acer and young Mitch visibly relaxed. Then, they dropped into 'downs', Acer with a soft groan between Britta and Sumi. "Yeah, my sentiments, exactly. You've got the easy part, though." But she paid notice. Her pack did not consider Sheriff Reid a threat. Unfortunately, she did.

Surprised by a second visit from him, Jessie wasn't prepared for it—not mentally, not physically. And, with her dad and grandparents gone to town, and John somewhere out on the property working a group of pups, she'd have to face this alone.

She stepped to the door, all dogs rising and padding along with her. She took a steadying breath, then opened it.

The sheriff who was headed up the path to the house turned at the movement, his hand reflexively moving toward his holster. Then, just as quickly he relaxed and touched the brim of his Stetson®—the same shimmering silver-white one. "What can I help you with today, Sheriff Reid?" she called, forcing a smile she didn't feel into her voice and onto her face.

"Came to return some of your property," he answered. Walking back to his vehicle, he grabbed an electronic clipboard and a bag from the passenger seat and walked over to her, handing her both as he sidled in to stand towering over her. Jessie resented that. She considered herself tall at five-foot-nine. As tall as her dad, he made her feel like a shrimp where her dad didn't. She didn't know why.

"If you'll sign for them …here and initial here." His finger indicated the spots on the device.

Checking in the bag, Jessie saw three of her four external drives with their connectors.

"I'll check them for damage, first," she said, heading back to her office. Mitch, Milo, and Acer got up, Reid turning to eye them as they padded by. Milo and Mitch pushed through between them to lead while Acer went to her left knee and glued himself there. The dog looked up, his eyes steady on the man who was looking down at him. Jessie saw admiration in Reid's face. Acer maintained his neutral, distant mien that was usual with those he didn't know. "This way," Jessie said to break the moment.

In her office, the dogs sat themselves down on their rugs, except for Acer who stayed with her. Jessica plugged in the drives, checked the numbers, accessed a couple critical files, and nodded. "Okay," she said, and got up. "They look like they're in the same condition as when they left my possession. I'll sign."

Reid handed her the electronic clipboard, but, this time, kept his distance.

Signing on the spots indicated, Jessie handed the clipboard back and, uncomfortable being under his scrutiny, stepped away from him and headed for the door.

All the dogs followed. "What about the rest of my property?" she asked once they were outside.

"Still being held in evidence, I'm afraid."

He actually sounded apologetic, though Jessie doubted his sincerity. "For how long?" she asked.

"I think you know the answer to that," he said quietly.

Yeah. She did. Probably forever. A sigh escaped her, and she saw him notice. "Well, thanks, at least, for returning these."

"You're welcome. And I want to thank you for that enhancement you provided on the thumb drive you gave me."

So he'd finally noticed that she *had* tried to help. "You're welcome." She expected him to go, but he kept standing there, just staring at her. "Is that everything, Sheriff?"

He took a step back and seemed oddly startled. "Yes, Ma'am." He touched his hat brim again, said "Good day to you," then turned and walked back to his SUV.

Jessie waited till Reid's rig disappeared down the drive before letting her guard down. Then, enervated, she went to the house, the dogs trailing in with her.

Plopping down on the sofa, she watched them settle around her—her dogs, her team, her pack. Oso and Queenie came over and put their noses on her. She gave them strokes. Then came Milo and Mitch. Last came the GSDs. She gave them all strokes in return for their sympathy. They always knew when she was distressed. And Jessie wanted to cry. Out her drones and her laptop with its expensive software, her entire five-year business model was thrown out of whack, and she didn't have a clue how to re-think it. All the work she'd done of securing individual permissions from local landowners to fly over their properties, of getting her FAA commercial licensing to fly the drones, of petitioning the State of Idaho, whose answer she was still awaiting—all that work down the tubes. Now she had to rethink everything. Or get another loan to buy more drones, which she didn't want to do. She needed a better business plan, one like her grandfather had pushed that only involved dogs. But that meant selling them to others, and that's what she didn't want to do. She needed to come up with something, though. Somehow. And she knew no 'somehow'.

Grabbing a throw pillow and hugging it to her, she tipped sideways, landing her head on the bolster with practiced habit. The sun glinted through the big floor-to-ceiling picture windows, dust motes dancing. One of the family cats walked through, stopped to look at her, then changed direction, threading its way nonchalantly through the now snoozing dogs to join her. It jumped up, curling itself into the cove of her abdomen. Idly, Jessie gave it strokes, and it started to purr. The sound soothed her. She closed her eyes and tried to put her mind on what she needed to do—find a new way forward.

*

REID GUNNED IT, meaning to. What he'd really like to do was get out and run off his anger. Instead, he took it out on the Anderson's private road, thankful for the luxury to do that—a mile-and-a-half of well-maintained road. *Better than the county ones*, he thought with both envy and discouragement.

He'd embarrassed himself. Standing there staring at her like that, analyzing her. But he needed to analyze her. He needed to know how she figured in this whole case. Especially since she had been in law enforcement—considered a valuable asset by both her captain and the Blaine County undersheriff, the latter who was himself nationally recognized, one of the few recognized as the top CSIs west of the Mississippi.

Remembering the girl of just a few days ago—cautious, but confident and composed—compared to the hollow-eyed, stiff, defiant hag he'd seen today, then comparing that to the girl he remembered from high school—every one of them completely different creatures—made him wonder if she was bipolar. Or maybe worse. Could PTSD cause schizophrenia? he wondered. Something was really, really off.

"She's not a girl," he muttered, power-sliding on the gravel through a hard curve.

The law enforcement choice for a career really threw him. Girls like Jessica Anderson didn't go into crime fighting. They went into tech, maybe. Even law like he had tried to, but on the corporate end of things. Heck, he could even see her as a successful CEO for some big corporation, especially with her dad's connections. But she was certainly not and never had been law enforcement material. That would have been her twin sister.

The old psych studies held pretty true, in fact. Cops and criminals held very similar personality traits on the MMPI, the standardized psychometric test of adult personality and psychopathology used by most institutions. Jessica didn't fit, but her twin sister did, and, true to type, Jennifer had flirted with law enforcement—literally—but had become a criminal, instead. Jessie? Never. Neither cop nor criminal. Just not the type. At all.

"I don't fit the profile, either, though," he said aloud, steering his way out of trouble when the rig's rear end lost traction. And he knew he didn't. But he had other incentives for what he did. Law enforcement was a family heritage dating way, way back, and a continuing tradition for every male since then. It was expected.

"No. Not true. Demanded." Again, he gunned it, and, again, the rear-end tried to slide away on the gravel. "Oh, no you don't," he muttered, bringing it back under control.

What he had wanted to do and what his dad and granddad expected weren't actually *that* far apart. At least that's what he'd thought. He'd thought wrong, though. Pursuing law wasn't in the cards for him, not if he wanted to live up to the Reid legacy. That had been made perfectly clear when he'd won a three-year full ride scholarship to go on to U of Penn Law upon graduating from ISU. He'd been forced—coerced, actually—into turning it down. He still resented his folks for that, mostly his mom who, to this day, had a feverish passion about the prestige of 'her men' wearing a badge. "Perverted," he muttered, thinking of her continued fawning over the family's collection of all the badges previously worn by Reids, badges dating all the way back to 19th century Scotland. "Just plain sick." But his anger was defused, and, inside, he simply felt sad—sad for himself, sad for Jessica Anderson, because, if he had to, he'd push the law to hold her feet to the fire. If he had to.

He took his foot out of it and coasted as the pentagon-shaped arch and two giant stone dog statues that framed the entrance of the Anderson place came in sight. The county road was just beyond. No more fooling around allowed. No more anger.

What bothered him most about Jessica, he realized as he headed toward civilization, was the change in her that had occurred in just the last few days. She'd gone from healthy-looking to haggard, like she'd aged ten years from doing hard labor in some third world prison camp. What had happened? And it crossed his mind that, maybe, somehow, it was his fault …which was ludicrous. She was the one who had failed to follow the law, and she would have *known* the law, because Colorado had the identical law and the same consequences for what she'd done, or, more accurately, *not* done.

Her attempt to hedge had displayed that fact. So did her silence concerning that hedge—tacit affirmation. She had purposely failed to report a crime, something she knew could put her away for a full five years.

***

14 – Motivation

A HAND SHOOK HER. "Jessie, wake up. It's dinnertime,"—her dad.

Jessie woke like a bolt of lightning had struck her. "Oh, *no*! I didn't mean to fall asleep."

Her dad chuckled. "Wash up, Jessie. Food's on the table."

"I haven't fed, yet."

"It's all done," her granddad, Darby, said. "Including those mutts you call dogs. That one big galoot," he said, tipping his chin in Milo's direction, "thinks he's a lap dog, I swear."

Jessie gave him 'the look', as her dad called it. Then, when he winked, she grinned. With a groan, she got herself up and into the downstairs bathroom. In the mirror, she saw her hollow eyes, dark circles ringing them. She hadn't been sleeping well since the sheriff confiscated her property—property that had taken the last bit of her savings and a loan from her dad.

Her hair was a mess. With her fingers, she combed it back, but it didn't help much. Then, after applying some cold water to her face and scrubbing her hands and arms, she headed to the table.

"You've decided what you're going to do," her dad said, stating it like fact as he shoveled potatoes and gravy onto his plate, then helped himself to some chunks of pot-roast. "Toss me a roll and pass the veggies, would you, Dad?" he called to Jessie's granddad.

Jessie watched Darby toss two rolls simultaneously, and her dad catch them both. Then her granddad picked up the vegetable bowl and, with a grin, threatened to toss it like a game ball. She watched her gram smirk and shake her head. This is what she'd missed being away all those years wasted at school, then a year in the worse purgatory of working as a rookie deputy. This was her family, and she still ached from missing them.

Jessie wondered, yet again, how her father always knew. "I think so. I think I dreamed it."

"Eat, Jessica Marie," her grandmother urged, and Jessie served herself as the dishes came her way. It was the first time she actually felt like eating since they'd taken her drones and laptop.

"Then it was a productive afternoon for you," Darby put in. "What did the sheriff want?"

So her granddad had reviewed the property surveillance. "To return three of my external drives."

"And the rest?" Oli asked.

"No go."

"Right. And?"

"I'm going to take Mitch, The Marvelous, and Milo, The Wonder Mutt, to California to meet Callen Parker at his place and give him a demonstration. I'm hoping to get him to certify them and my method, and to agree that a dog doesn't have to be limited to just human remains detection."

"You're not thinking of driving, are you?" Ana-Mari asked, concern saturating her grandmother's face and voice.

"Yes."

"No. Absolutely not, Jessica Marie."

Oli held up his hand. "I'll fly her and the dogs," he said. "That will solve that."

Both her grandparents nodded approval, and Jessie sighed in relief. They always worried …like flying was safer or something, which it wasn't, not to Jessie's way of thinking.

"When do you plan on going?" Darby asked. "We've got the government boys coming in June to pick out their dogs."

"I'll have to call Callen and see if he'll even give me the time of day," Jessica said.

Her dad smiled. "He will. He knows you, and he knows our dogs."

While that was true, Callen had very high standards and his tests were tough. He was *the* authority for scent tracking dogs. He was even recognized for his expertise overseas, and, while she was now a budding somebody herself in the world of search and rescue, she was still a nobody, even a beggar, in the world of Human Remains Detection or HRD. It was Callen who had given her a leg up by putting his stamp of approval on her method just last year after testing Queenie and Oso, and she hoped he'd now be impressed by Mitch and Milo, too.

A phone call later netted Jessie her answer. Yes, Callen would see her and agreed to test Mitch and Milo, both, and, most importantly, as a team, in HRD. That was huge. Jessie felt as if the shadow that had cloaked her since discovering the body up on Long Peak had finally lifted. "I look forward to seeing your dad, again, too," Callen added. "You will stay here, of course. My wife and I would love to have you."

"Sure."

"Good. And tell your dad to bring me a pup as good as the last one, and I'll even think about coming up there the next time you need to recertify."

And there it was—her only real 'in' was her family's rep. Everything was always about Anderson Working Dogs. "I'll be sure to tell him," Jessie said, her eyes flicking to her father who was listening in on the other line. "And thank you."

"Let's just see what you can do before thanking me, shall we? See you on Tuesday next."

When the connection closed, her dad chuckled. "Of course he wants another pup. And I've got two, one GSD and one Malinois. He likes them dumber than a post, and play-oriented. Well, these aren't dumb, but they do have what Callen calls 'prey drive' and means 'play drive'—a lot of motivation to just 'go, go, go for fun'—

too much for our training. They don't stop and think first. Just jump in."

The words came out fast and furious, her dad spitting them out faster than bullets. Jessie started to chuckle, tried to smother it, couldn't. She knew what he actually called them—brain-dead—though not really meaning it.

Stormy brows met her laughter, and she swallowed in a hiccup and tried her best to sober up. Didn't work, but his brow quirked. She took a breath, and that steadied her. "What will you charge him for them?"

"Same as I charge pet buyers."

"So, these are culls?"

Her dad gave her a scolding look. "None of our dogs are culls, Jessie. Even the ones that aren't up to our standards are good, beautiful, smart dogs. Just not suitable for serious work. Too happy, so too dangerous once their prey drive or their defense drive is fully engaged."

"You're talking about the one you call Chip?"

"Yep. That one, and Boyd. Maybe a couple of others. Whatever he doesn't want, the SAR group down there will."

Jessie shook her head. "I don't know why SAR and HRD people prefer hyper."

"It's because the dogs are easily fixed on one objective, Jessie. Lots of 'go'. Easy to train to one goal and one goal only. Let's be honest, not many people, even pros, are willing to go to the lengths we do, and especially not the lengths you do."

"Yeah, I know. I just disagree."

"I know you do. That's why I support you in this. Smart, thinking dogs perform best. It's why we breed the heritage lines. It's something we all agree on, including your granddad."

Darby nodded in the 'darned right' way he had.

Her grandfather and she didn't agree on much when it came to dogs—neither she and him nor she and her dad. They were all about dogs as working assets. For her, dogs were partners …teammates—part of her pack, and she part of theirs—and that's where her dad and her granddad wouldn't go. "Too dangerous," was their reason. But that's all they would ever say. No substantiation for their position, just grim looks and compressed lips.

*

NOBODY HAD SEEN Debbie Ferris. She hadn't shown up for work. Her coworkers hadn't seen her. Neither had anyone in her contact list. There'd been no online activity, and her sister, who lived down near Boise, hadn't heard from her. That wasn't unusual, they were told. "Debbie kept pretty much to herself. We haven't been on speaking terms for several years," she'd told Red.

Upon asking the girl about the whereabouts of their parents, she clammed up, and Landon thought that worth pursuing. They finally tracked them down over in Lemhi County, but they had no listed phone.

Barry contacted the Lemhi County S.O. and asked them to do the interview, emailing over a list of Landon's and Red's questions.

The source of the money was eluding them. With over twelve grand in play, it couldn't just be from dance tips. The truck was also drawing a blank. Tracking down every red pickup built between 2007 and 2013 that was registered in the county proved tedious and time-consuming, but not difficult in a county whose population was barely sixteen thousand, most of those living in either the county seat, Northridge, or one of the other small towns and unincorporated villages. Unfortunately, not one of the vehicles they managed to find, all but about a dozen registered, matched the dents and paint scars seen in Jessie Anderson's enhancement of the fleeing vehicle's hood, driver's side, top, back, front, and bed. Regardless, pictures of all of the trucks were catalogued, their owners interviewed.

They moved on, engaging the departments of adjoining counties. Meanwhile, interviews with both Sue and Debbie's friends and coworkers netted a list of activities and confirmation that both were, indeed, in a relationship with one another.

Barry shook his head. "That can't have made her family too happy."

"Oh? Why's that?"

"Got a call back from Lemhi S.O. They knew she was homosexual, and, ah, they don't approve of it. Kind of sticklers about it, in fact. They have their own church. Not part of any recognized denomination."

"Right."

Landon started to head back to his office, stopped when a hunch hit him square in the forehead, turned around, and said, "Barry?"

"Yeah?"

"What are the chances that our perp killed Sue *because* she was homosexual?"

The man didn't even hesitate. "Doubtful."

"Why?"

"We just don't have that kind of extremism here."

"What if we do and just don't know about it?"

If the flesh on a man's face could suddenly loosen up and physically droop, that's what Landon swore happened at that moment to Barry's. "I—I can't even imagine…." Barry shook his head. "Good people live here. They may be old-fashioned, even fanatic in some cases about their beliefs, but they're not …capable of doing what happened to Sue. No way. Not in the Bitterroot."

"Well, somebody is."

"Got to be somebody from outside," Barry said, and Landon could see he was resisting the idea.

"What if what we have here *is* a hate crime and the killing has just started?"

"Then we'd have a problem, sir."

And a possible motive for our killer. "Have somebody pull all the missing person files going back five years and have them delivered to my office, would you? I want to follow a hunch."

The man looked skeptical, but said, "Will do."

***

15 – Flight Trauma

GETTING MITCH AND MILO accustomed to flying proved a very noisy experience. Milo kept shaking his head, whining, and rubbing his ears with his paws. Mitch just howled the whole first test flight.

"Maybe I should just drive," Jessie said.

"Call the vet," Oli suggested, but, when Jessie did, the solution was sedation, something she was loathe to do.

"Can we try again?"

"Sure. Let me get my earplugs."

The second time up wasn't nearly as bad, but still not good. Jessie went to a different veterinarian—a woman who had just moved down from Alaska and who had a reputation for seeking cause, not just reaching for the standard treatment protocols.

"First, I want to take a look in their ears, then maybe do an x-ray."

Half an hour later, both Mitch and Milo bounded out of the clinic area all wags, and Jessie had a diagnosis. Milo had tiny Eustachian tubes. Mitch? Just nerves or, perhaps, Dr. Kathy Caldwell suggested, he was sympathetic to Milo's misery. "They're very bonded," Kathy noted.

Jessie smiled. "Yes, they are."

"So here's my suggestion. Diphenhydramine for Milo—what you probably know as Benadryl®—and valium for Mitch if necessary …which, if Milo responds well to the antihistamine, may not be necessary. Can you take another test flight?"

"I think my dad would, *maybe*, suffer it again."

"Would he allow me to come along?"

"I suppose. Misery loves company, and all."

Kathy smiled. "My thought is that, if either or both show distress, seeing it would allow me to better diagnose a potentially effective remedy. And, of course, I can alleviate their discomfort and your dad's in moments with a quick-acting sedative."

Jessie nodded. She really liked this woman. "Okay. I'll ask. When would you be available to do this? We're kind of running out of time."

"Let me check my appointments."

They scheduled it for the next afternoon, but they needn't have. Milo pretty much managed with only a couple of headshakes, and Mitch settled down once Milo did. "Take doggy chews with you so they can keep clearing their ears. But I think they're going to do fine."

Jessie agreed. Dr. Caldwell had found the cause and affected the perfect solution. Now all that was left was to go inform the sheriff.

*

"WHY DO YOU HAVE to okay it with the sheriff?"

"Technically, I don't, Dad. It's a courtesy."

"Jessie, I never, ever agreed with your choice to go into law enforcement. You know that."

She did. *But you're okay with the military for Erik*, then frowned as she realized that she was still angry about her older brother's decision to become a SEAL like her father.

"I play nice with them for business reasons, but I don't respect many of them. Known too many bad ones—criminals with a badge, a bunch of hooligans licensed to kill. Give them an inch, and they'll not only try for the country mile, but the whole territory."

That was true for a lot of different occupations, especially business. But, yes, it was there in law enforcement, too. It had certainly been evident in the attitude of some of her fellow deputies in Blaine. But it wasn't *her* attitude, and, because she knew the reason for that attitude, she knew how to defuse it …or thought she did, anyway.

"Let's get your lawyer's take on this, first, okay?"

"Already did," she said. And she had. He'd agreed with her.

"I don't believe you."

That made Jessie step back. Her dad had never, *ever* called her a liar before. She felt something break inside, and it hurt. A lot. It also made her angry, because she had never, *ever* lied to *him*.

Her mom? Yes.

Her sister? Definitely.

Her brothers? Maybe.

Her dad, granddad, or grandmom? Never had and never would. The most she would ever do would be to keep silent unless they asked her a direct question. Then, no matter what, she'd answer them honestly.

Fixing him a look, she took out her phone, hit Pearson's picture, and, when it connected and started ringing, she put it on speaker.

"Hogalby and Pearson."

Her eyes steady on her dad's, his on hers, challenging her, she said, "This is Jessica Anderson. May I speak with Mr. Pearson, please. It's important."

"One moment, Ms. Anderson. Let me see if he's available."

Moments later, Pearson's voice came on. "Jessica? What's up?"

With a sweet smile in her voice, she said, "I have you on speaker for my dad's sake, Mr. Pearson, because he just called me a liar." At that, she saw her dad drop his head. "So, if you'd please answer honestly for his benefit: Did you agree that it was best that I advise the sheriff that I plan to leave the state for a week?"

Audible through the phone was an intake of breath. "Hello, Oli. And, yes, I did advise that to be the best course considering the circumstances. It demonstrates Jessica as a cooperative potential witness."

If a man such as her father could squirm, he would be doing so now. "When did she become a witness?" he asked, his voice gruff.

"The moment her property, and, therefore, she, through her property, surveilled a felony crime scene."

Her dad leveled accusing eyes at her. "First I've heard about it."

"Jessie?"

"Yes, Mr. Pearson?"

"Haven't you told your dad what you're potentially facing?"

Of course she hadn't. "…Mmm, no."

"Maybe it's time you do that."

Jessie thought about it. Didn't want to. Knew he'd find out eventually. "Okay, Mr. Pearson."

"I'd like to hear how it goes with the sheriff before you leave, all right?"

"I'll call with the details."

"Good. And, if I forget to say it, have a good trip."

"Thank you."

When the connection terminated, Jessie stood watching her father, waiting for some sign. He, in turn, sat watching her. He gave in before she did, also pretty much a first. "Well?"

He's not going to like this. "Well," she began, "it's what Sheriff Reid mentioned. Idaho Code Section 19-4301A—Failure to Report. I could face a fine of ten-thousand dollars and five years in prison."

The frown descending her dad's face was one she'd only seen a few times in her life, and never had it ever been directed toward her. It was, now, though. "Explain," he commanded.

Jessie sat down, and took a huge breath, trying to decide how to approach it. Straight out, she decided. "Because I'm a certified CSI, because I have a degree in criminal forensics and an associate's degree in criminal justice, the fact that I witnessed what they deem I would know, by virtue of those degrees, plus my time as a sworn deputy, to be a felony crime scene and did not immediately report it as such, makes me guilty of violating the law. It's circumstantial, but it would be hard to convince a jury or a judge, if I chose a bench trial, that I *didn't* know."

Her dad was ever so slightly nodding his head up and down, up and down—the merest suggestion of movement. His eyes had gone hard, glittery, and sharpest blue. His face had gone to that curiously expressionless poker face that Jessie knew harkened back to his time as a Navy SEAL. "Did you know?" he asked, his voice so soft that the question was barely audible.

But Jessie heard. "Yes."

*

REID WAS SIPPING HIS THIRD CUP of bad coffee, still working his way through last night's activity logs, checking the status of those arrested and those simply detained for their own safety, when, once again, Red poked his head around the door of his office. "Incoming," he said.

Landon looked up to see a deputy pushing a rolling cart laden with two boxes down the hall toward his office,

Red standing back to allow the man past him. "What's this?" Reid asked.

"What you asked for. The unsolved missing person reports from the last five years."

Startled, Reid had the man unload the boxes against the wall behind the visitor chairs—one full of clasped files, one half full. "That many?" Reid asked. He couldn't believe it.

"Yep," Red replied. "If you want help, do give out a shout," he said. Then, as he left, tossed, "Not that anyone will answer," back over his shoulder.

Getting up, Reid tentatively unsnapped the catch and opened the cover of the top file in the nearest box. A couple a sheets of paper, a picture, some hand-written notes—that was all that was in it. "Oka-aay." He grabbed a handful and returned to his desk, pulled the top one, and began to read. Then, he read the next and the next. There wasn't a whole lot there. These were the oldest.

Two hours later, he finally found one with something to bite his teeth into—a case that went back two years. The missing person was a young woman—Lily Thompson. She was in her twenties when she went missing, the daughter of a well-known family. A known lesbian, she was reported missing by her partner, a woman named Sheila Simpson. She'd disappeared after leaving work at the The Club Cafe where she worked as a waitress, the same place Sue Bigsby had worked. *A connection? Or just coincidence?*

He read on.

No trace of her whereabouts had ever been found. Sheila Simpson disappeared a week later, but she was found by the FBI. She'd moved to L.A. without so much as a word to anyone.

The next one he found happened two months after that—a woman in her thirties named Frieda Bates who worked as a court stenographer. She had failed to appear for work, and, when Northridge P.D. officers went to her home, they found no vehicle and the neighbor taking care of her dog. The neighbor claimed that they took the dog because it hadn't been fed or watered in two days. They'd called animal control about it, but nothing had been done.

Talking to Frieda Bates' workmates netted them the fact that she was a Methodist. One of the other court stenographers said that Frieda had mentioned that she thought she was being stalked by a guy in a red pickup.

"Yes!" Landon grabbed more files out and dug in.

***

16 – Courtesy Call

"THERE'S A JESSICA ANDERSON here to see you, Sheriff. She insists she'll only speak with you and won't state the nature of her business."

Jessica Anderson. Just who he *didn't* want to see. Not with the mess of going through old missing person's files piled around everywhere as he tried to find evidence for his hunch. Still, there was nothing for it. "Go ahead and escort her to my office." Landon's eye caught again at the craziness of his unkempt office. "…Wait." Then, with a sigh, he shook his head. "…Yeah. Bring her here."

"Yes, sir."

But the woman who walked in wasn't a Jessica Anderson he recognized. Smartly dressed in heels and a tailored suit, her platinum blonde hair coifed like she'd just stepped out of a salon, the woman who walked in a few minutes later was confident, in charge …together—like a VIP corporate CEO. He stood up. "Ms. Anderson," he said. "To what may I owe the pleasure of this visit?"

"This is a courtesy call, Sheriff Reid. I'm advising you that Dad and I are flying down to California for business. We plan to be gone a week, starting tomorrow and, weather permitting, we should be back by next Wednesday."

"I see. Sit down, Ms. Anderson."

She eyed the chairs—one filled with files, the other loaded with more files. "Let me get those," he said, scooping up the pile from the nearest chair, his intent that of stashing them …somewhere. He looked around, desperately searching for some place safe to put them other than on his desk to get mixed up with the ones he was reading.

His movement was too much for the disorganized stack, though. It promptly shifted, the slick file folders sliding sideways despite his attempt to pin them with his chin.

Anderson's hands reached and caught at them, steadying them, as her laughter broke loose. "Must be the week for it. My hanging files just jumped out of their frame in my filing cabinet yesterday. Let me help."

She grabbed the top of the stack and stashed them on the floor near the cabinet where her drones were locked up. He followed suit with the rest that he still held clamped tight in his arms. "Thanks," he said, instantly grumpy.

"Obviously, I caught you at a bad time."

"So how about lunch?" He said it out of the blue, his own mouth never warning him of what it was planning.

"Sure. Dutch, though."

He hadn't heard that term used except by his grandmother. He faked it. "Don't know that place. How about The Hereford?"

"Steak for lunch, Sheriff?" she asked, tipping her head and grinning.

"And for breakfast and dinner, too, if possible."

Again, she laughed.

Who was *this* woman? And he seriously considered the possibility, rare as it was supposed to be, of dissociative identity disorder. "Let me get my hat."

*

"I'LL HAVE THE SPECIAL," Jessica Anderson told Jeremy, their waiter.

"Yes, Miss Anderson. Would that be medium, as usual?"

"Yes, please."

"Sparkling water?"

"Yes, please. With a lemon twist."

"Yes, Miss."

Landon blinked. So she was a regular here. They knew her personally. And her tastes. Why hadn't he seen her here before, then.

"Sheriff Reid, sir?"

"Yeah. I'll have the same, but just knock the horns off, and wipe its butt. And give me a couple of extra rolls, would you?"

Jeremy chuckled. "Yes, sir. Something to drink?"

"Coffee with cream."

"My dad says that—knock the horns off, and wipe its butt," Jessica said after their waiter left. "Must be a man thing."

"It's something my dad always says, and I've just continued the tradition."

"Tradition is good."

"Sometimes."

She gave him an odd look, dropped her eyes and gave a little nod as if to herself.

"What?" he asked.

"Hmm. I was just thinking that some traditions need to be …retired."

"For instance?"

"Oh, I was just thinking about my older brother. I got a call from him this morning. He's a SEAL, just like Dad was. He went in, because, well, I think it was because it's what he thought Dad expected. And Granddad, too, maybe. Something military, though Darby was a Master-of-Arms in the Navy, not a SEAL."

"I don't think they had SEALs back in your grandfather's time," Landon said dryly, "but you don't think Erik would have done it otherwise?"

She turned her head to face him. "Actually, I think they did have SEALs when my granddad was in the service. The SEALs started in 1962. How do you know my brother's name?"

"He was in my high school graduating class. We played football together."

"Oh." She looked away, her eyes going far away for a second. "Right."

Her sparkling water arrived, and she took a sip. "So you're heading to Cal, huh?" he asked.

She nodded. "Dad's flying us."

"Call me nosy, but what for?"

"I'm hoping to impress Callen Parker, again, this time with Milo and Mitch for human remains detection, what we in dogs call HRD. They're both doing really, really well for me."

He nodded. "Don't know of this Parker you mention, and don't know much about anything dog-related. Horses are my thing. And cats."

"Callen is one of the top experts in canine SAR and HRD both in the U.S. and overseas."

"I see. So this is a good thing if he gives his stamp of approval."

"Oh, he already has on my SAR methods. HRD is a whole different thing, though."

"Well, I can see, with your credentials, that, yeah, his sanction would work well for you, maybe."

She gave him a look that was just nigh short of peeved, then said, "You know all about me, don't you?"

"I know what's a matter of record. You did it to yourself, you know. Not my fault you were flying your drones that day. But that's got nothing to do with the conversation, does it? What's Callen Parker do for you?"

She seemed to weigh his response, then said, "HRD is a closed shop. Just like SAR is, now. You have to be a first responder, or retired from it, and know how to handle evidence to even play."

And now, finally, he had his answer. Now he knew why she'd gone into law enforcement and into criminal forensic science. He chuckled, happy with the knowledge. Now it made sense. "Search and Rescue is, yes. Human remains? Well, there are very few resources available here for that kind of work. Most finds here are accidents, a skull found by a hunter or hiker. It *is* a shame about search and rescue, though. But it's because of lawsuits. Gone are the good old days of just putting out the call and the community gets out there with their dogs and horses and finds our missing people. In fact, I miss that."

Her head jerked his way, her blue eyes turning even darker blue, if that was possible. "What?" he asked. "Did I say something you disapprove of?"

"Not at all. It surprises me to hear you say it, though."

He sat back, rubbed his tongue across his lower teeth as he contemplated her words.

"You're law enforcement," she said when he didn't respond. "You, as sheriff, *are* the Authority Having Jurisdiction, or AHJ, as my professors called it, making you one of the most powerful law enforcement entities in the country. I don't expect that kind of perspective from law enforcement officers—any of them, much less the AHJ. They're all into power and control. Keep it in-house and under jurisdictional authority."

Those words almost bubbled over themselves in their rush to be said, and Landon heard candor—rare from anyone. What she said was surprising to him, coming as it did from someone who'd been boots-on-the-ground in law enforcement herself. She knew The Code, but hadn't been seduced, then indoctrinated, by it, and he didn't know quite how to respond. To admit that he might agree could make him vulnerable. To not admit it might alienate. He didn't like either option. Luckily, their food arrived.

*

FINISHED WITH LUNCH, Jessie went ahead and let the sheriff pay the bill, putting up just enough of a fuss to seem legitimate. Outside, she let him walk her to her vehicle—her gram's fancy Lexus, borrowed just for this occasion. Then she nodded and smiled as he touched his hat and thanked her for informing him of her trip. He wished her well, and he seemed genuine. Jessie thought that, all in all, the meeting had gone well. That remained to be seen, though. She'd find out soon enough.

Waiting until the sheriff got into his rig, she watched until his unit turned onto the highway and disappeared in traffic. Then, she dialed Pearson's office and told him, in detail, of the meeting, backing up her report by sending an encrypted, zipped file of the audio to him, all perfectly legal in Idaho, a one-party consent state upon which, at the onset of the two-plus hour recording, she had, of course, recorded her consent. The lawyer was pleased, said he'd listen to it and get back to her, then again wished her a successful trip. "See you when you get back. Good luck on your endeavor."

"Thank you."

Home, she returned the smart key to the Lexus to her grandmother and went to her room. Closing the door, she kicked out of the heels, stripped out of the fancy clothes and hung them up, then got into her jeans, boots, and a tee. Bathroom next, she brushed the gel out of her hair and washed off the makeup. Then, grabbing a jacket, she went out, saddled up Chesterton, let her mare, Snake, come along, running loose, and spent the rest of the afternoon out on the trail, the dogs coming with, free to explore every scent they found delightful.

She needed the break, and so did they. Mostly, she needed to get her mind completely off of her upcoming test with Callen Parker now that she'd taken care of appeasing Sheriff Reid.

***

17 – Surprises

SITTING IN THE CO-PILOT'S SEAT in her dad's G58 Baron, Jessie watched, admiring his efficiency as he ran up the engines at the end of the taxiway and went through all his before-takeoff rituals. Seeming satisfied, he called the tower and requested clearance to runway one-zero, and, minutes later, they were airborne, the ground falling away beneath them.

In the back, both Mitch and Milo, along with her dad's four young dogs, lay in their crates, completely relaxed, contently chewing on their rawhide bones. Jessie let out a long sigh of relief when they hit altitude with not so much as a whimper out of any of the dogs. So far, so good. Only about three hours to go, then to make it through landing without Milo's ears causing problems.

"You fret too much," her dad said. "That Benadryl® trick is a real winner."

"I just hope landing is as easy as taking off once Milo's ears adjust to our altitude."

"Let's not make problems for ourselves, okay?"

"Okay."

The day was beautiful, and the weather report indicated they'd have clear skies and calm weather all the way. Still, Jessica, who trusted her dad and his flying, didn't enjoy placing her trust in a machine—never had. Not even cars. She liked her feet on the ground or her butt on the back of a horse. Machines could break, and something breaking when at an altitude of up to 15,000 feet was not Jessie's idea of a good time. Still, in all the years she'd been flying with her dad, nothing bad had ever happened, and today was a beautiful, clear day.

"What are you thinking, Jessie, my Jessie?"

"Just that it's a beautiful day."

"Right. That's not what you were thinking, at all. You were fretting."

Jessie grinned at him. "Well, I've got a test coming up tomorrow. You don't. So I can fret if I want to."

Oli laughed. "Okay. Fret away, but, while you do it, chew on this. Darby and I want to make you a full voting member in the business."

Jessie felt her stomach do a flip. She turned in the seat and faced her dad.

"Dad suggested it, and your grandmother and I both agreed. Our lawyer has drawn up the paperwork. It's ready whenever you decide to accept."

Jessica felt like the whole world had just shifted. And then reality seeped in. "What about Erik? I thought he—"

"Erik is on board with this."

Jessica frowned. "When did he tell you that?" He certainly hadn't mentioned it in his phone call to her.

"In February."

"Oh." So, as usual, she was the last to learn about everything. Well, not last, but, of the dog people in the family, for sure. Her sister and younger brother—well, one had no legal right to an interest in anything, having been summarily disinherited, and the other had more pressing issues, like trying to stay alive and healthy. "Can I think about it?"

"Is there really anything to think about, Jessie?"

Yes, there was, actually, but she didn't say that. "I guess not."

"Good. We'll wait until this trouble with the sheriff is out of the way, of course."

"Yeah."

And suddenly the full impact of what her family was offering hit her, and she just about lost it. Blinking back the tears that threatened, she whispered, "Thanks, Dad."

He grinned. "You earned it a long time ago, Jessie. Unfortunately, you weren't old enough then."

And, yeah, once she was old enough, she'd gone her own way. If she had known….

*

THEY'D BEEN LUCKY. Idaho State Police Forensic Services, the ISPFS, had put a rush on their samples.

And unlucky. Their perp was not in the database.

The truck was still their best hope, but, so far, that had turned up nothing. It was like the vehicle didn't exist, yet they knew it did. What Landon had found in his research through old cold cases of missing persons was that it had first appeared two years ago, and continued to be identified in three of the more than twelve more recent cases.

"Fourteen! That's a lot of potential victims," Barry said, coming in with some paperwork. He stepped closer to the whiteboard Landon had up.

"Yeah, it is. And where are they?"

"You think they're dead and up on Long Peak?"

"I don't know. You'd think that, if they were, somebody would have run across something, though. Skulls, lower jaw bones, hips, femurs…."

Barry scoffed. "I don't know that most hikers are actually that focused on their surroundings, really, though. Mostly they're focused on getting to their destination."

"Yeah. I know. Still, though, we get a lot of tourists traipsing around these mountains, never mind hunters and trappers. You'd think someone would have tripped over something. But you didn't come in here to listen to me grouse. What do you need?"

"I don't need anything. I come bearing gifts."

Landon frowned, immediately suspicious. The last time Barry had brought him a gift, it had brought down the ire of the county commissioners. "Let me see."

Barry grinned and handed over the papers he held.

Scanning them, Landon looked down the list in column one, then down the list in column two, noting the disparities. "Where'd you get this?"

"I set it up. Assigned a couple deputies to visit all the local car dealerships, new and used, and got them to share their sales reports for pickups since 2007, which is when the 2008 came out. Then I went back to the DMV database and tracked down every one I could. I had Lara do title searches on the state level to make sure they hadn't been sold as scrap. That's the result."

And a lot of work. "Remind me to give you all a raise," Landon said. "This is really useful."

"I've got deputies and reservists out checking the ones that aren't registered, since we've already checked everything that is and came up empty handed. Hope that's okay with you."

"Do you really have to ask?"

Barry grinned. "Nope."

Landon stood up and stretched. It was lunch time. "Let's go find us an early lunch, shall we? Then I want to go visit Martin."

Barry let out a long sigh. "Can't. I've got a doctor's appointment at noon, and I'm on strict orders not to eat or drink anything until after."

"Gads, man. I hate those tests."

"Tell me about it. You going to warn Martin you're coming?"

"Nope."

"Don't know if that's wise. Last time I went to visit without giving him a heads up, he was about as friendly as mad badger, as Sam likes to say."

"I'm forewarned."

***

18 – Veteran Perspective

MARTIN DOYLE WAS SITTING in a nice lounge chair letting the sun bathe him through the window of his rehab room. "Hey, Martin," Landon said, taking his hat off and plopping down in one of the couple of visitor chairs available. "How are you feeling?"

The older man scowled at him. "How would you be feeling? First, it's like you're being tortured and asked to do things even an Olympic athlete couldn't, then, alternately, you're treated like some old geezer, not even allowed to go to the bathroom by yourself without permission."

Landon stared down at his boots, reached down to brush at an invisible scuff mark, then shook his head. "I wouldn't." He looked up and grinned. "I can break you out, if you want."

Martin groaned. "Don't think my wife wouldn't come after you, Landon."

"Hey, I can still run fast."

"Except she's a crack shot."

"Yeah, well, there's that. Speaking of it, how *is* the shoulder and arm?"

Martin grimaced. "Getting there, but it's slow."

"Still not right?"

"Not yet. Three surgeries worth. They tell me no more surgeries, but lots of therapy and I'll get almost full use back."

"Almost?"

"Yeah. There's some scar tissue in the shoulder they're worried about."

"Hurt?"

"Not bad."

"Say, you remember the Lily Thompson case?"

"Missing persons," Martin said. "While your dad was still sheriff."

"Yeah. That's the one. And how about Frieda Bates?"

The man perked up. "That one I took a personal interest in," Martin said. "Never found her. Never found the other one, Lily, either. We turned 'em both over to the Staties who then turned it over to the FBI. Last I heard about it."

"Yeah, and that's where it still sits today. I saw your notes in the Frieda file. Why'd you take a personal interest?"

"She was a court steno, a member of my church, an upstanding citizen, volunteered as an elections clerk, plus she was a wonderful Sunday school teacher. The kids loved her."

"Was she gay?"

Martin gave him a stare. "Not that I know of. Never saw her with anyone. She had a dog and a canary. My wife's got the canary still. Neighbors have the dog."

"So, not gay and wasn't seeing anyone of the opposite sex, either?"

Martin chuckled and shook his head. "Landon, I'd say she was just one of those women who men don't find very attractive. Not that she was ugly or anything. Just …well, normal—old-fashioned normal, that is. Came from good upbringing—one of those women who has 'spinster' branded on them from the time they get to high school."

"Didn't wear her hair weird or look like an Emo- or Goth or whatever was the fad a couple years ago?"

Now, Martin laughed outright. "In our courts? Honest? …No, Landon. Never. Not Frieda. She was a very conservative, nice young woman who sang in our church choir."

"Right."

"Why all the questions about her? Weird questions, I might add!"

"I've got a murdered suspected lesbian, and her partner is missing, too. A red, older model, unlicensed truck is involved."

Martin sat forward and his eyes went sharp. "When?"

"Week and a half ago—April 7th. ME puts her dead on the 6th. Got no match on the DNA found on and in the body."

"Where'd you find her?"

"Up on Long Peak. She was raped, strangled, and her body mutilated, then left on the bank of Long Creek between the upper and lower falls area. Got footage of the perp and the red truck."

That made Martin really sit up and take notice. "Footage?! You got an ID, then?!"

"Can't identify him from the footage. He's wearing some sort of mask. Most we know is he's got dark hair, about six foot, slim, and drives this darned red pickup we can't locate."

There was a long pause, Martin's face going pensive. Then: "How'd you get the footage?"

"A woman testing out her new drones caught it."

Martin gave a long, soft whistle. His hand—his good hand—went to his chin. "That was lucky for you. ...Except for the masked part, of course. Obviously smart, then." He paused, then said, "So it all comes down to this red truck, which could be a coincidence."

"It could be," Reid agreed. "But the truck we have video of has no license plates, front or rear. And it's a 2008. That's what your interview notes say was true about the one that neighbors saw and that Frieda told her coworker was stalking her, right? That make, no plates, and about that vintage."

"Yeah."

Again Martin's hand went to his chin. A frown creased his brow. Then, suddenly, he looked up. "You know, there's this Special Needs kid," he said. "…Well, he was a kid when I first met him. He's got to be in his …ah …closing on thirty, maybe, now. Anyway, he goes out and takes photos of people's cars driving on the highway and county roads. He's got some form of autism, I think, and he's real OCD, so we pretty much ignore it."

"You mean Robert Tandy?"

"Yeah. That's him. You might go ask him to see his photos. Maybe he got a snap of someone driving that truck in his collection."

Landon wanted to groan, but didn't. "Okay. Thanks, Martin," he said, getting up.

"Hold yourself right up there, Landon. You're not getting out of here that easy."

Reid frowned. "What?"

"I'm coming back to work, thank you very much. Enough of this laying around and getting ordered about. Help me get my clothes on. I'm signing myself out of here, and you're giving me a ride to base."

Reid laughed. "So you *do* want to get me killed."

"Huh?"

"Your wife?"

Martin grinned. Got a twinkle in his eye. It was the liveliest Landon had seen him in his whole convalescence. "Well, that would put me in charge, now, wouldn't it? Not some still wet behind the ears legal beagle who only won the election 'cause of his last name, his rugged looks, and fancy hat."

Reid eyeballed his undersheriff. "You mean the same one who kept his opponent on as undersheriff?"

"Same one. And if you're that worried about getting shot, then put on some Kevlar®. Dorothy always aims for center mass. Taught her myself, I did. Now get me my pants and shirt out of that closet. And grab my boots. We've got work to do, the first being going to visit Robert."

***

19 – Special Talents

ROBERT TANDY LIVED in a group home on 3rd Street. He worked as a night janitor at the Grover Elementary School. Diagnosed as mildly autistic, he seemed relatively normal, except for his extreme OCD. The man—he was in his thirties, now—had to have routine and insisted nothing ever be in the 'wrong place'. His four Special Needs housemates mostly shared his OCD fetish. They were grouped that way on purpose.

The house was run by a husband and wife team trained by the state to manage clients like Robert Tandy and his cohabitants. "Nice," Robert told Landon and Martin, tipping his head toward them. "They cook good food." He refused eye contact.

Explaining what they were looking for—a 2008 red, single cab Chevy 1500 truck with no license plates—both Landon and Martin held their breaths waiting for Robert to respond.

Suddenly, the man got up and headed to and then up the staircase. Landon and Martin watched him go, and, one, am hungry, though, and you're welcome to join me, since there's more than enough for both of us."

Her dad fought it, then gave it up, a grin breaking out despite his peevishness. "Your idea?"

"Gram's."

He shook his head, his face relaxing, took two sandwiches, a couple of packs of string cheese, and one of the thermoses of soup, then plopped himself down on the tarmac.

Jessie did the same.

"Sorry to spring it on you about the business, but—"

Jessie shook her head and frowned, stopping him with a raised hand as she swallowed her bite. "Don't be sorry. I kind of knew something was up when you all went to town last week." Then she asked what she really wanted to know. "Did you mean what you said about me, though? That I earned it?"

Her dad's face got that gentle look that always made her want to hug him. "Yes. A long time ago. You've got something special when it comes to dogs, Jessie, my Jessie. You've always had it, even as a toddler—you and the dogs all around you. It really is like you communicate with them on some unknown level. More than that, though, you've got the skill, the work ethic, and the know-how. You're a hard worker and not afraid to take on huge projects, things I'd even balk at, like getting those permissions from the owners to fly your drones over every piece of private property in Idaho—"

"A work in progress."

"And asking the state for a waiver to the law."

"Also a work in progress."

"Yeah."

She flinched inside a little at asking something else she really wanted to know. Taking a breath, she plowed on. "When I came home at Christmas, you told me that you thought I needed help. You still think that?"

A look that Jessie always thought of as his eyes sparking flitted across his face. "I think you need to heal, and the *best* way to do that is to keep busy and work doing what you love."

So, he does. It hurt. "Idle hands and all that, huh?"

"Yes."

"But no therapy."

"Waste of time, money, and, in all honesty, I consider it destructive, at least the kind of counseling most of those weirdos practice. I swear most of them are psychos themselves."

Jessie laughed outright. "That's actually evidentially accurate. Just like cops are criminally-minded."

"*You're* not criminally-minded."

Jessie nodded. "I know. And I'm not a cop anymore, either. Even back in school, I wasn't given a very good score for success in my psych evals. I don't think like a criminal, so how can I outfox one? That's the measure."

Her dad blew a hard breath out. Shook his head. "Just wrong," he muttered. Then, "Jessie, what happened that you finally *did* come home? You've never said."

Jessie concentrated on her sandwich. Finishing it, she poured herself some soup. She set the lid down to let it cool, folded her hands in her lap, and raised her eyes to his. "Do you remember spending all that time teaching me how to defend myself while I was growing up?"

Oli nodded.

"Well, self-defense against someone who is trying to kill you is, I found, pretty straight forward, whether hand-to-hand, or with a weapon."

Again, he nodded.

"But …I don't know how to describe it. There's a difference between people who are actually attacking you, and people who want to *hurt* you. There's this feeling of maliciousness, of evil, and they *like* that evil. It's like they're filled with …hateful glee at the prospect. They're rabid. A rabid pack of animals. Nothing human. Nothing hu*mane*. That's what ate into me as those men came at me. It was gruesome, nasty, mean, violent glee. They were enjoying terrorizing us. I had to wait till they were close enough. Down to seven rounds in my last magazine. I could see their faces. They were actually enjoying the prospect of killing me and the wounded men Acer and I were protecting."

She felt tears rolling down her face. "Dad," and she was sobbing, now, and hated herself for it. "I can't handle knowing there are actually people in the world like that. They *like* viciousness. I just can't handle it. I may have studied it in my psych classes, but nothing, *nothing*, prepared me for …for *that*."

They watched him type in his password, his fingers surprisingly deft. Moments later, he opened up an app and clicked on a red square, clicked on 2008, and, when that opened, clicked on a clipart rendition of a truck. "There," he said as the screen began to fill with photographs of red trucks—small pickups all the way up to semi-tractors and dump trucks.

Fishing out his phone, Reid pulled up the stills they'd captured from Jessica Anderson's video enhancement. Then he started to compare.

Robert looked at the picture Landon had up, reached out a finger and swiped to the next one like an expert, then the next. Grunting, he started scrolling through his pictures on the laptop with surprising speed, stopping occasionally, then moving on.

Screen pages later, the man stopped, looked again at Landon's pictures, looked at the ones on the screen, and said, "This one."

Reid and Martin both bent in. "How do you know?" Landon asked.

Robert Tandy pointed to the rear bumper. "That deep scrape gouge." Then he pointed to the grill on a front view. "And those teeth are missing."

Looking closer, Landon saw that Tandy was right. The missing grill teeth weren't significant, but the angled gouge on the bumper was.

Tandy then opened a drawer and pulled out a thumb drive. He proceeded to pull the photos over onto it, the computer burning copies to the little device. When it had completed the job, Robert pulled the drive from its slot and put it on the desk near Martin.

Getting up, Robert Tandy then went to his wall and pulled out a particular binder—one that looked identical to all the rest. Opening it, he paged through, then popped open the binder's rings and pulled out five stiff pages mounted on both sides with 35mm originals of the scanned-in, digitalized photos. "You can make copies and then bring me them back," he said. "The negatives are in the little white packets slipped in between the mounting cardboard, too, if you need those. They are all labeled."

"Are you sure it's okay for us to take these?" Landon asked softly. "I know they're valuable."

Tandy nodded. "It's okay. Martin Doyle is my friend."

"Okay. We'll get these back to you right away. Thanks, Robert."

"You're welcome."

Robert Tandy walked them out. Never once did he or had he made eye contact or gotten close enough to touch, not even to shake hands.

*

LOCATED OUT ON THE RIVER, Callen's place was modest and very unassuming—at least it seemed that way when you drove up. Inside, though, the house was a lot bigger than it looked. Spacious and comfortable, airflow was immediately noticeable. So were dogs—Callen's dogs. All six—two GSDs, two Labs, one Golden, and one mutt—sat patiently as Jessie came in with Mitch and Milo. At Callen's nod, they approached, one by one, as he pointed to each, greeting the newcomers with cautiously wagging tails.

Immediately, Milo went into play mode, forearms flat on the ground, butt in the air, tail wagging furiously. Mitch, much more conservative, soon realized these were cohorts and relaxed his inborn reticence toward canine strangers. "You can let them off lead, now, if you want," Callen said.

When Jessie did, all eight dogs did the nose to tail thing, again, this time as a group, then disappeared around a corner like a gang of kids intent on making for the playground.

"Do your dogs know how to use a dog door?" Callen asked.

Jessie laughed. "No, but they know how to open human ones unless they're locked, and then even, sometimes, when they are. I'm sure they'll figure it out."

"I'll show you to your rooms. Then, Margaret is setting up a tea on the patio," Callen said, his arm extending. "This way to your rooms?"

The room Jessie was taken to had its own bathroom with a shower. Stashing her carry-on and equipment bag in the closet, she went to her dad's room and knocked on the still open door.

His room was similar to hers. "Yours have sliders going to a small garden sitting area?" she asked.

He opened the curtains. "Yep."

"Wow. Lap of luxury and all that."

"I guess. If that's what you're into."

"I'm not, but, still, it feels like V.I.P. treatment, doesn't it?"

Her father laughed. "I guess so."

Somehow, his answer peeved her. "I suppose you're used to it."

He grinned. "Yeah, pretty much. Nothing much impresses me, anymore, Jessica. I find that, usually, the more ostentatious, the more the jackal."

"Callen's not like that."

"I know he's a good guy, Jessie. But Callen Parker is the exception to the rule."

Finding their way to the patio, Jessie met Margaret Parker, a woman who was what Jessie thought of as typical 'queen mom' material—thick in the waist and conservative in dress with a friendly demeanor and ready smile. Like Callen, Margaret spoke with a decidedly English accent. And the 'tea' Callen mentioned wasn't just cups of a hot, brewed beverage, but rather a light meal of what turned out to be delicate meat sandwiches, a pudding, and delicious sweet cakes.

Jessie wasn't quite prepared for what Callen sprung on her as she bit into a bun Margaret called a 'Sally Lunn'. "I took the liberty of inviting a few friends over for the actual trial, then dinner tomorrow night after it," he told both her and Oli. "Thought it would be delightful if Jessica could elaborate on her proposed changes to search and rescue techniques, specifically that involving multiple dogs working under one handler."

Jessie looked at her dad who was busy slathering clotted cream and jam on his second sweet bun. He took a bite, saw her watching him, and gave her a wink.

"Just a few chairpersons and team leaders. Oh, and a president of one of the national organizations of which I'm a member."

Callen glanced at Oli's frown, then put his eyes back on Jessie and smiled. "Hope you don't mind."

***

21 – Trust

THE DAY DAWNED BRIGHT and sunny with temperatures in the sixties. Mitch and Milo were both feeling happy and confident, which was better than Jessie felt.

She hadn't slept well the night before, not just because of nerves about the upcoming test, but mostly because of Callen's bombshell announcement. Jessica felt 'on the spot', and she wasn't prepared. She didn't have any of her tracking results. Those were all home on her drives, the files too huge to easily transfer by someone back at home. Nobody there was computer savvy enough.

Heading out for her morning run with her dogs, her dad surprised her by joining her, his pups trailing him. "Thought we'd see Callen's estate, since he invited us to," Oli said. "Maybe try to find that trail through the scrub oaks he said leads down to the river."

"Uh-huh."

"What's up, Jessie, my Jessie?" her dad asked.

"Nothing."

He pulled up short, his dogs milling about his knees until he told them to '*sitz*'. Jessie stopped, too, Mitch and Milo both downing. Jessie gave them the okay to go explore, and they did. Then she pulled up a piece of ground, sitting down cross-legged. "I'm ill-equipped and ill-prepared," she said.

"For the test?"

"For the dinner talk."

"Just be yourself," Oli said.

"Are you responsible for this?"

"Nope."

"You didn't say anything to Callen about that test you and Granddad saw?"

"Nope."

"Is it my turn to disbelieve you?"

That seemed to jolt him a bit. "Nope. And I'm very, very sorry I challenged you about your honesty the other day, okay? My bad."

Jessie sucked in a deep breath. "Forgiven."

"But not forgotten."

"It's the first time you've ever doubted me. It shocked. Worse, it hurt. A lot."

"I know. And I don't …and didn't. Doubt you, that is. Not really. This whole situation of you facing felony charges threw me. Just threw me. …Jessie, I'm sorry."

She shook her head, unable to quash the smile that broke on her face. Somehow, all her hurt and stress just seemed to vanish into thin air. She felt better than she had in days. *So, this is all about my father's trust in me? Wow.*

She got up. "I love you, Dad." Then, unable to stop herself, she added, "…But not enough to let you beat me down the hill." And she took off, Mitch and Milo bounding out of the scrub to join her.

*

CALLEN WAS OUTSIDE with his dogs when they came back from their run. He waved them over. "Are these my pups?" he asked.

"Well, they're the ones I brought for you to pick from," Oli answered. "Of course, you're not obligated."

"Mind if I play with them a bit?"

"Not at all. Be my guest."

Squatting down, Callen introduced himself to the pups. They seemed to take to him immediately. "They speak German?" he asked, looking up at Oli.

"Yes."

"Good."

"*Hier*," Callen called, taking a few steps.

The dogs looked at Oli, then at Jessie, then back at Oli. "It's okay," Oli said softly, using the key word 'okay' in a very specific way.

When the pups still looked dubious, Jessie turned to Mitch and Milo. "You want to go with them?" She raised her hand in Callen's direction, but only as a question, not a command, and her dogs knew the difference.

The dogs looked at her, looked at Callen, then, Milo deciding, Mitch on his heels, the two of them trotted over to the pups, nosed them, then bounded over to where Callen stood still encouraging them. The four pups followed.

"How in the world do you do that, Jessie, my Jessie?" her dad asked, admiration clear.

She turned pensive eyes his way. "I'm as much at a loss as you are. I have no idea. Maybe it's just because we're all such a team, now."

"Well, whatever it is, it's priceless. Think they'll be okay if we disappear for an hour?"

"Oh, sure. I left my room open. Their dog beds and chew toys are there, plus their kennels and their woobie blankets. They'll be fine."

Then, let's go find us a shower and go out to breakfast, shall we?"

Jessie felt dubious about it, much as she really would love to escape Callen's domain for awhile and get her head on straight for the upcoming ordeal. "What will Callen and Margaret think?"

"That we went out for a dad and daughter breakfast," Oli said with a laugh. "I told them last night after you went to bed. There's this breakfast joint I go to every time I'm in town. You'll love it. They make your favorite."

"Eggs Benedict?"

"To die for."

That sealed it.

*

AFTER GETTING THE PHOTO LAB to put a rush on reproducing and enhancing Robert Tandy's photos from the negatives, Doyle and Reid grabbed four deputies to help them, including Lieutenant Red Wheeler, Dave Kins, Regina Larson, and Lara Somners. He handed out thumbdrives with Robert Tandy's digitalized versions, then spread out the full color prints on a sticky white board, all of the photos blown up way larger than the originals. "We've got to get every match possible to the man in this truck," Doyle said, taking a pointer and circling the driver. "I know it's not much to go on, but it's all we have."

They spent hours going through driver's license photos in the Idaho Transportation Department database. "Too bad the ITD doesn't take photos of people the way they usually dress!" Lara said finally with an exasperated sigh. Then, looking over at Reid, added, "Like you and your cowboy hat, or the guy we're looking for in his."

Landon couldn't help himself. He started laughing. It caught on and the whole group of them wound up laughing themselves breathless. "What's going on in here?" Captain Barry Olmstead said, walking in bearing some paperwork for Landon to sign.

Landon waved him over, glanced through the documents, signed, then said, "Lara just cracked us all up with a pertinent point. Whoever would recognize somebody looking all flat faced and pouty, sans hat or whatever else they usually wear, but are made to strip off when we take those driver's license photos?"

"Oh." Barry frowned, though, then, pointedly to Lara: "The *point* is to get a good frontal face shot."

"And how many people do you know resemble their driver's license photos?" Lara asked him just as pointedly. She took hers out and held it up next to her face. "No resemblance."

It was true. Landon didn't even want to think about his. Didn't look a bit like him. Not really.

Barry shook his head, muttered something, then stalked out.

It was Lara who also wound up solving their problem. She went out to the bathroom, ran into Sam Hull, and towed him back with her. "Look at these, Sam," she said, pointing to the blow ups of Robert Tandy's originals. "Who is that driving?"

Sam looked, stepped closer to the board, stepped back, thought a moment, then declared, "That's ol' Hugh Buford. Maybe 'bout ten years ago, or so."

***

22 – The Test

MITCH AND MILO MET THEM at the door, the four pups, plus Callen and his dogs coming down the hall to greet them. "I want them all," Callen called. "They're marvelous! Simply marvelous."

"Thought you'd like them," Oli said. "But *all* of them?"

"Every one. I could use eight more, to be honest. My group's dogs are all getting up in years. These are good pups, perfect for the job and smart, too. Lots of drive."

"Eight?" Oli looked dubious. "Don't have that many like these, sorry."

"But you will, right?"

"Usually get one or two in every litter."

"Put my name on them, if you would,"

Oli nodded. "I'll keep you in mind."

"That's all I can ask. But let's make it official. I'll put a reserve payment on them today, so you don't forget."

Oli laughed. "Not necessary."

"And I say it *is*," Callen replied, frowning. "I'm very serious. These are very, very good dogs. I want first dibs."

Then Callen turned his attention to Jessica. "And I envy you your two here. I'd swear they understand what we're saying."

Jessie smiled. "They seem to, almost, don't they?"

"My staff has the test prepared. I'm afraid I've made it rather difficult, but I'm sure you and your dogs are up to it. Now, we're just awaiting our guests. They should be here at ten."

"I think I'll go lie down for awhile, then, if that's okay?" And, calling Mitch and Milo, Jessie escaped to her room, there to fret.

*

"TIME TO GET STARTED," Oli called with a knock on her door.

"Coming."

Surrounded to either side by Mitch and Milo, Jessie asked them to get down. Both dogs raised their heads, then flipped, belly up, into 'cute' mode, tails thumping, mugs grinning, eyes full of humor.

It was the usual ritual. She snapped her fingers and pointed 'off'. In their usual ritual response, they ignored her, reclaimed *her* pillows with their heads, thereby forcing her to extract herself from between the covers that their bodies pinned down around her and scoot herself off the bed over the foot. Only then did they relinquish *her* pillows and bound—Mitch—and step down—Milo—off the bed.

Their clowning around brought a smile, just like it usually did. It was a good ritual.

Running a quick brush through her hair, she looked from one dog to the other, flipped them a treat, hugged Milo, stroked Mitch, and, with a quiet, relaxed confidence, she grabbed her pack and opened the door. She was ready. So were the dogs.

Her dad waited there, shoulder leaned into the wall. He grinned, seeing her, shrugged himself upright, and said, "You look great. Guess the nap worked, huh?"

Jessie laughed. "The dogs worked."

"In your dreams?"

"With their cutsies."

"Hmmph. Yeah." He looked down at them. "The cavorting cavaliers. Let's go. The ogres are waiting."

"Ogres?"

"Bunch of sourpusses. I've been sitting in on their conversation with Callen. Really full of themselves, they are."

"Nice."

"If you say so."

"How about 'usual'?"

"That I'll buy."

Outside, Callen stood with a group of five people, faces she recognized from SAR newsletters and Internet mug shots. Introduced around, she shook hands with one and all, barely hesitating despite her repugnance for the ritual. "Callen seems to think a lot of you," Elsie Poindexter, the present leader of a small but influential SAR group, said, "so, when Doug told me about this, I invited myself. Hope that's okay with you."

Jessie nodded. Doug was the head of one of the big, national organizations. "Of course," she replied, smiling. "No problem." It was a lie, but she wasn't about to make a fuss about the woman's presence. Nor anyone else's. This was her show, but she wasn't in charge of it. Callen was.

"Shall we get started?" said their host. "This way."

"One more question. How old is the Malinois?" asked Doug Ingalls.

"Almost a year."

One of his brows arched and his lips compressed. "That's way too young."

Jessica heard Callen blow a long breath out his equally long nose. "This is not a standard test. This is my test of this woman's method. You were invited because I thought you'd, perhaps, find it illuminating to see some experimental methods in the field. Now, if we can get on with it?"

It was the first time that Jessica had ever heard Callen Parker move from his typical, very English *noblesse oblige* to an irritated, even temperamental 'haughty'. She was grateful.

*

CALLEN EXPLAINED THE TEST to her, the observers listening in. "Forty acres, a total of thirty scent placements of varying sizes and levels of decomposition, some of which are animal remains to throw them off. Two of my staff have also laid track, then hidden themselves to try to distract the dogs."

Jessie nodded, listening. "Synthetic or real human remains?"

Callen looked startled at her. "Real. Why do you ask?"

"I've only trained with synthetic. I'll be very interested to see how they do when they experience the real deal," Jessie said.

Callen frowned. "I've never had much luck training that way," he said. His eyes spoke 'dubious'.

"Well, let's just see how they do," put in Elsie.

Jessie smiled. Her sentiments exactly. She was excited by the prospect.

"I don't see rubble or even a ladder or slide, though," Jake Dawson said. He was the leader of an urban SAR team.

"This isn't an urban HRD test. It's a test of Jessie's method and her dogs. As I mentioned, she's got a unique program. It's that I'm testing."

"Oh. Okay."

"What's th—"

"Please. Let's get on with the testing. Questions may come later."

"Can you at least give us an overview of what we'll be observing?" Doug Ingalls asked.

Callen turned to Jessica. "Miss Anderson?"

Taking a deep breath, her nerves suddenly kicking up, again, Jessie faced the group. "My dogs work as a team. They work the entire field at will. Once they alert, I go to their position, drop a marker where they indicate, then stay there until another alert indicates my need to attend."

"Well said," Callen congratulated. "Let's begin." He looked at his watch, raised his hand. "In three …two …one …mark."

She sprinted toward the sound, which was coming repeatedly from within the scrub oaks. She almost tripped over him in the deep brush. "Good, good Milo. Sorry about that. Clumsy humans, and all."

He got up once he'd pointed to his 'find', watched her drop the marker, then, ducking his head, threaded his way through the thick bushes to the west.

Jessie followed and started at a young man squatting by a tree. "Oh!"

"Hi. Completely ignored me after one glance," he said.

Mitch's alert interrupted them. "Off I go," Jessie said with a grin.

And so it went. Jessie was winded and sweat-soaked by the time she knew, by the numbers, that they'd found them all and not too many. Milo's bark …barks—insistent. Then a howl. …Repeated howling. Jessie ran. She couldn't see him. The howling continued. She heard someone's footsteps behind her—the young man she'd met briefly in the woods.

Spying Milo's white body, Jessie broke through the brush to see him bouncing up and down, up and down, another howl resounding. "*Was? Was ist los?*" she asked.

He whined. Sat. Looked through a chain link fence. Stuck his head up in the air and howled, again.

Mitch came running up. Nosed Milo. Looked beyond the fence. Then he, too, began to bounce and bark.

"Callen, there's a problem. We're at the western boundary—the highway fence," Jessica heard the young man say.

She turned to look at him. He had his phone to his head and was obviously in communication with her host. "He's indicating another 'find'. Actually, both of them now are. They're insistent. …Outside, on the highway side of the fence."

"That's not fair!" Jessie said accusingly. "I call foul."

"We didn't—" The man listened. "Callen's coming."

Actually, everybody came, including her dad. By that time, though, Jessie had decided. She was pulling a piece of tarp out of her pack when they all came running up.

She threw it on the fence as Callen said, "What are you doing?"

"There's something out there," Jessie said. "Both of them say so, and I trust them." She turned on him, still angry. "I told this to your man, here. This is not fair, and I call foul."

"Robert? Did you—"

"No. I swear. No tricks."

"Hup," Jessie called, leaning her weight into the fence to make it stable. Milo bounded over the four foot barrier. She looked at Mitch, then, and he bounded up, Jessie catching and steadying him, as he boosted himself over, too.

"Jessie," her dad said, stepping up. He cupped his hands, and, using them to give herself a leg up and over, Jessie followed her dogs.

The whole slope down to the highway was weedy grass, all mowed short, but still green. Milo downed at a slight dip of disturbed ground. Mitch sat, then bounced. Both dogs didn't bark or howl anymore. Jessie was already there. She stared at what, repeatedly, they pointed at with their noses—nothing apparent, but she had a bad, bad feeling.

She turned toward the crowd now standing on the other side of the fence. She began to shiver, despite being flushed and sweaty. "I think you need to call 9-1-1. I think there's someone …or thing—" She heard her voice falter, and paused. Took a breath. "I think there's something human buried here."

***

23 – Skeptics

"IT'S PROBABLY JUST CRAP," Elsie muttered as they waited for authorities to arrive. "Homeless people do that, you know," she said, directing her gaze at Jessie as she said it. There was disapproval written all over the woman, in her voice, in her expression, in her body language.

"They don't usually bury it," Callen observed dryly.

"Whatever."

Jessie realized the woman was scorning her dogs ...had scorned the entire demonstration. The rest probably had, too. It saddened her, but she'd expected it. But this made the idea of giving a presentation at dinner even more nerve-wracking.

*

IT TOOK SACRAMENTO COUNTY AUTHORITIES almost an hour to get there. Once they did, they made short work of snapping a couple of photos, then getting a shovel. Moments later, though, the officer digging stopped. "Call the coroner," he said to the deputy with him. Then he looked over at Jessie. "We'll need your statement."

Jessie had her eyes on what they'd uncovered. Her dogs had been right. As always.

*

NATURALLY, SAM HULL had been dead on. Sure enough, in the DMV database there was a red Chevy truck listed as belonging to Hugh Buford, purchased new in 2008. A visit to Hugh—in his eighties, now—yielded them a "Yep. Gave it to my nephew a handful of years back," he told them, giving them the man's address and phone number. "Go easy with him. He's kinda simple, y'know." And all the specifics Hugh gave them matched what they'd tracked down via the truck's vehicle history, too. But, supposedly, the nephew had sold it to someone else, though the present title was still in the nephew's name, despite the release of liability that had been filed.

"Could be a ruse," Barry said. "You should take backup."

Bringing four backup units, Landon himself approached the nephew's house, all his nerves taut. The man—a heavyset fifty-something came out of the house as Reid got out of the car. "Can I help you, officer?" he asked, no hedging, and a face as readable as a young kid's.

Landon relaxed somewhat. The man was in tight jeans, cheap sneakers, and a t-shirt, despite the April chill. There was no bulge of a knife or gun apparent. "Are you Kenny Buford?"

"That's me."

"You have a red pickup?"

The man frowned, said, "Yes," and pointed to the two-year-old Ford Ranger sitting in the drive right next to the house. The truck was cherry colored, not red.

"I mean the 2008 Chevy 1500 you got from your uncle, Hugh Buford," Landon said.

"Sold that when I got the Ranger," Kenny said.

"To whom?"

"Ah.... Don't remember the guy's name. I think I've got it somewhere. Don't throw much out around here, and it's old habit to keep copies of everything."

"I'd appreciate it if you could help us out on this," Landon said.

"Sure." The guy motioned to him. "Come on in."

Landon glanced at one of his deputies—poor Kins, again—and motioned for him to join him. The young man trotted up, and they both followed Kenny Buford into his house.

After half an hour of rustling around through papers on and in a desk, then rifling through a big, metal filing cabinet, Kenny Buford finally let out a yelp of glee. "Found it!"

'It' was a photocopy of both the title, filled out to the buyer, and another of the release of liability Kenny had carried down to the local DMV. Attached was the receipt and proof of release of liability he'd gotten from the DMV for his three-dollars-and-fifty-cent fee payment.

"You remember what this 'Bernard Jones' looked like?" Landon asked, reading the name—the same name they'd turned up on their search of the records—a name, physical address, and mandatory Driver's License number, none of which existed. It was something the DMV should have caught in this, the computer age. It hadn't.

"Uh…." Abruptly, Kenny sat down on the edge of an overstuffed chair. "Ah, sit. Sit," he said, extending his hands out, palms downward, then flapping them a little. "I got to think back."

Landon watched the man frown, creases forming between his brow and on his forehead. The blue eyes went far away, staring nowhere. Then the man's face shifted. "…Yeah. Tall guy. Skinny. Real white skin, real dark brown hair. I remember him looking through the glove box, then under the seat. Wasn't too concerned about the engine or nothing. Didn't care about the dents."

Hugh shifted his eyes to Landon's. "I used it to haul wood, and, you know, you get dents when you do that."

Landon nodded. "Anything else you can remember?"

Again, Kenny's eyes got that distant look. "He smelled funny—kinda like…." The man actually sniffed, several times, inhaling as if he could remember the smell that way. "…Dirty socks or something," he said finally. Then, after a moment, he said, "And he had real funny eyes—absolutely gray. Not pale blue. Gray."

"About how tall compared to, say, me or Kins, here?" Landon asked softly.

The man stood up. Looked sideways toward the wall, then slightly up. He brought his hand up. "He was about like this," he said, holding his hand about ten inches above his own head. "What's that? Six-two, six-four?"

So a little shorter than me. "How about age?"

"I don't know," the man said, not engaging in any of his previous 'remembering' routine. Instead, he shrugged. "Not young. Not old. Maybe in his thirties. Could have been younger, could have been older. Not a good judge of age. Sorry."

They had a description. It had been a long time coming, and it wasn't much, but it did match the few bits they did have—Jessica Anderson's video captures from her drones.

"Would you be willing to look at pictures when we get some to show you?"

"Sure would. Just give me a call on my cell phone."

"And that number is?"

The man rattled it off, and it matched what Landon had in the notes on his phone concerning Kenny Buford. "Thanks. Might be a day or so before we get them together."

"I'll be here. …And come there," Kenny said with a grin. "Save you the drive." And Landon blessed the fact that Kenny Buford was gifted with a magnificent memory for physical details, even if how he accessed it was a bit on the strange side.

*

"IF WE GO NOW, we'll have just enough time to go over your results, Jessica," Callen said once Jessica had finished filling out the requested paperwork for the sheriff's deputy.

"Did they tell you what it was? I couldn't hear," Elsie asked.

"It was a decomposing fetus or neonatal human corpse," Jessica said as her dad lifted her bodily over the fence after Jessie boosted Mitch back over, Milo making the leap all by himself.

"You mean a baby?!"

"They won't know if it was pre- or postnatal until they do an autopsy," Jessica replied. "Chances are from the brief glimpse I caught that it was a stillbirth, though."

"It's still a baby."

"If we could leave the day's unpleasant disruption behind us, please," Callen said. "We've only got a couple of hours before the caterers arrive, and I think my staff have everything set up for us in the living room."

A fifteen-minute hike back to the house, then bathroom breaks, put them in the now darkened living room. "Robert? If you'd get the lights and start the show?"

"I usually will pull only the most exciting parts, but we're just going to speed through the visual record as I share my thoughts," Callen said as the videos began playing, one on the main screen, with it and seven others playing in small insets to either side. "Here we have the beginning where Jessica is instructing her dogs. Interesting hand signs, I must say. I expected the dogs to begin casting, but they didn't—not immediately. Then the big one begins after surveying the field, but the smaller—the Malinois—he stands and surveys a lot longer. Only then does he begin."

Callen fast forwarded, then suddenly switched to a video from a different viewpoint, running it at normal speed. "Now watch closely as the dogs methodically move. I was instantly intrigued. There wasn't any randomness here. It was an amazing piece of calculated teamwork between the two of them. If we switch to camera 3 and 4—Robert, if you would—we can clearly see this."

"How long did it take them," Doug Ingalls asked. "And what are their numbers?"

Callen stopped, looked around the dim room, then, raising a hand to Robert, the video flipped off and the lights came on. "I'm going to assume that you're not particularly interested in going through the details, so we'll just get to the statistics."

Callen handed out some photocopies of a hand-drawn map marked with checkmarks and time notations. "The dogs found every hidden sample—every one, plus one—the dead infant outside the highway fencing. "They did so in just under fifty-two minutes, and I think they'd have been even faster was it not for them having to wait for their handler to come drop markers. Robert and Sandra—my helpers—indicated the dogs glanced at them when they came upon them, but went on their way, never straying from their assignment. All in all, an absolutely amazing demonstration."

Callen stood suddenly. "And, now, ladies and gentlemen, if you would all please join Margaret, my wife, on the patio for some lovely refreshments we've prepared, while Jessica, her father, and I finish some business to which we must attend."

They waited till the group had exited to the patio area, then Callen requested Robert and Sandra to break down the equipment and take it to "the inner sanctum."

"This way," he said to Oli and Jessica as his staff began to fold away the sliding partition that covered the wall-sized display screen they'd been watching. "Margaret, bless her, has provided us our own little tea in my den. She, as is her wont, anticipated this turn of events. I didn't. Unfortunately, we're still going to have to suffer through dinner, but, meanwhile, let's enjoy your huge breakthrough, Jessica. Just amazing work. Amazing. Of *course* you'll get my sanction. And I would like your permission to present this video record to the international association."

***

24 – Home

LANDON REID WAS RUNNING his stud horse through a reining pattern when he heard the plane overhead. Letting the horse stop and blow, he looked up and wondered if it was Jessica Anderson and her father coming home. Not many folks had planes that landed at their small, private airport. *Could be.* It had been about a week. *Hope she got what she wanted.*

And, for just a moment, he felt sorry for the girl. *Woman, darn it. She's no kid.*

"Just acts like one," he muttered, answering his own self-scold.

The stud horse gave a snort and tossed his head, then began pawing. Landon patted him on the neck. "Okay. Back to it, shall we?" he asked, nudging the horse into a lope with a touch of heel and lift of rein.

The horse stopped short mid-pattern moments later, his head going up, ears pricked as the snarl of a high-performance engine interrupted the pastoral quiet of Landon's small ranch. "What in the world—"

The engine stopped. Then, "Sheriff Reid?"

"Here," he called, recognizing his ME, Dr. Jerald Lorenson's voice. He dismounted and let himself out the gate, his stud horse giving him a shove in the middle of the back. "Duster, quit," he hissed as Jerald came around the side of the barn. The man looked excited. "What's up, Doc?"

"I just got confirmation back that what I thought I'd found in the autopsy is, in fact, what I suspected."

"Oh?"

"I have casts of the sizes and shape of both the left and right thumbs of whomever strangled Sue."

"…Wha— How?"

"From imprints on the skin on the neck and corresponding damage to the cartilage of the esophagus. There were no fingerprints—not surprising. We think the killer wore gloves, but the pressure was hard enough that it did leave evidence that I was able to get Meridian to determine thumb shape and size. The killer has thumbs in which the second phalanges are very, very long—just over an inch-and-a-half—and also which are very much wider than is common at the interphalangeal articulation between the first and second of the thumb phalanges."

Reid frowned, understanding everything up to interphalangeal articulation. "Could I have that in plain English, Doc?"

"Here," Jerald said, shoving an image at him. "We generated the size and shape from our findings. They look like this."

Behind Landon, his stud gave a small snort, then started rubbing his head against Landon's back, practically knocking him into Lorenson. "Sorry, Doc. Duster, *quit!*" Then, "This is good. *Really* good. Come in for some coffee?"

"Love to."

"Let me put the beast away."

*

BACK HOME AND ARMED with Callen Parker's blessing, Jessie decided to try the local 'sanctioned' search and rescue group. Led by a man named Nelson Remmers, his group was independent from any other organization in the U.S. and abroad, but it was him the sheriff's office called when there was the need for a wildland search—independent Idaho.

The meeting was scheduled for 7:00 P.M. in the county fairgrounds' indoor arena, a place Jessie hadn't visited since before she'd gone to college. Arriving half an hour early in hopes of catching Nelson or maybe someone she actually knew, she found no cars in the parking lot. Walking around to the metal clad building that housed the indoor arena and its bleachers, she found the place locked down tight and no note on the door indicating a last-minute change of venue. She decided to wait. *Maybe they all arrive nearer to seven*, she posited.

But seven came and went and still nobody showed up. Pulling out her phone, she dialed Nelson Remmers' listed number. And, as usual, got the answering machine with its curt, gruff-voiced message of "Leave a name and number" after an electronic voice dictated the number she had dialed. She'd already done that. Twice.

Her grandfather quizzed her when, back home, she walked in the door at eight. "How'd it go?"

"It didn't," Jessie answered. "Nobody showed up, and there was no note. Remmers' phone went to voicemail, as usual."

"That's strange."

But Jessie didn't think it was. What she thought was that the local SAR group was a closed club. They might post notices in the paper and online on their website, but those notices were probably bogus. They probably met at Remmers' house or something. She told Darby as much.

"Well, why don't we drive over there and see?" her granddad said, getting up.

Jessie just shook her head. "It's already dark outside. They'll have quit by now, anyway. Besides, it's almost bedtime."

"Come on, Jessica Marie," he said grabbing his hat, coat, and some keys. "Let's take the bull by the horns. Get in my truck."

*

THEY TOOK ONE of the official business trucks with its 'Anderson Working Dogs' signage and logo. "How do you know where he lives?" Jessica asked, getting in the passenger seat.

"Because he advertises that he sells dogs and that he's a trainer. …Like we don't."

"You know much about him?"

"Enough to know that he's not someone I want to rub elbows with," Darby said quietly.

"That doesn't speak well, Granddad," she answered just as quietly. Then, "How did he come to be recognized as the local SAR leader?"

Darby looked sideways at her. "The Remmers go back to World War I era here, Jessica. They aren't newcomers like our family."

Jessie shot him a look. "We're 'new'? We've lived here for what, two decades now?"

"And, in this country, that's still a newcomer. Idaho is like that, Jessica. You've got to live here for half a century to be taken as even a legitimate county resident. It takes at least two generations to become established, and, even then, the founding families still consider you an outsider."

Pulling into a ramshackle place on Fog Creek Road, Jessie saw lights and vehicles under security lights at a wooden barn. "I guess you're right, Granddad."

"Usually am."

As they got out, dogs exploded into a rage of frenzied barking that was more than just an intruder alert. "Wow," Jessica whispered.

"Yep. You be ready, just in case," her granddad warned. "Man's been known to loose them on folks."

A young man came out, looked, then went back in the barn's man-door. Moments later, a short, paunchy man in jeans, a blue plaid shirt, and a battered cowboy hat came out the same door. He pointedly shut it behind him as Jessie and Darby approached. "What can I help you with?" the man asked.

"Looking for the SAR group," Darby answered.

"Well, yeah. You've found it."

Darby gestured toward Jessica. "Granddaughter here went to the fairgrounds looking for your meet."

The man grinned. "We're a closed group," he said. Then he spit at the ground—an insult to them. "We don't need more dogs or handlers."

"Do you test?" Jessica asked, breaking in.

The man turned his face to hers for a moment, then looked back at her granddad. "When we need to. It's certification would still be honored, now. I'm told it's an insurance thing."

"You're FEMA certified," Ana-Mari said.

Jessie nodded. "But that's all urban disaster searches."

"And now by Callen," Oli put in with a grin.

"Yeah."

"And all that gets you where?" Darby asked.

"Nowhere in Idaho, I guess," Jessie answered, defeat coloring her voice.

She sat down with her plate, grabbed the maple syrup, and poured it over her French toast and sausage.

"Why? I'd think that would automatically qualify you to run a search and rescue operation," Darby came back.

"In another state, maybe. If I was a first responder, especially, but, like I said, not in Idaho."

"So, it's all on the county sheriff?"

"Yeah."

"Great! And you ain't popular with him, now. You'd have been better off staying in Colorado."

That was true. But Jessica hadn't wanted to stay in Colorado. Home was here.

"So, what's your plan, Jessie?" Oli asked, his voice soft.

"I don't know."

"I know you have one."

Watching her butter swim in the syrup, she took a breath and held it. Then she looked up. "I want dogs to work in packs—to autonomously move in search of the lost or dead. And that's what I'm trying to train for. But it's a three-fold battle. One is getting Idaho and other states to let me use drones, second is getting recognition for the method, which I've got a start on with Callen's blessing. The other is refining the training with my dogs, then repeating it with a different bonded pack. Over and over," she said. "And I want to go national, then international, with it."

"Whew!"—Darby. He ducked his head and focused on eating.

"Big dream, Jessie, my Jessie," her dad said softly.

"Yeah. Probably too big."

"Nothing is ever too big for the Andersons," Darby put in. "Nevertheless, this morning, we're tackling the Nelson Remmers problem head on. I won't be treated that way, and I certainly won't let Jessica be treated that way. He's a cad, a slimeball, and a shyster all rolled into one. Already talked to someone and got the fax back. Ana-Mari? Oli? Jessica? Get dressed for town."

"Not me," Ana-Mari said. "My 4H group is meeting here today at ten."

"Spoil sport," he sniped, grinning as he did.

"Trouble-maker," she shot back at him with a laugh.

*

LANDON REID DID NOT EXPECT to find Jessica Anderson, her dad, *and* her granddad all waiting for him when he got to the office at just after nine. "That's what I get for treating myself to breakfast out," he muttered.

Getting a briefing from the deputy on rotating desk duty, he blew a breath, then stepped out into the waiting area and motioned them back. "So, what's this about?"

"Search and Rescue in this county," Darby said, settling himself into one of Landon's two office chairs.

Jessica Anderson indicated the other chair to her father, then pulled up a piece of cold floor for herself amidst the still teetering piles of files. She lowered herself to a cross-legged sitting position, butt on the floor. Once she had, Oli Anderson then took the proffered chair.

"I'm speaking about one Nelson Remmers, in particular, Sheriff," Darby Anderson continued. "He showed us the gate when we went to inquire, and we know he isn't qualified like our Jessie, here, is. I'm given to understand that you're the man in charge of all of it, so Nelson Remmers has your say so, and, if I might say, *and I **will** say*, his attitude leaves a lot to be desired."

Rearing back at that tirade, Landon wished he'd called in sick and just stayed home. Settling himself against the wall, unable… un*willing* to sit when the lady in the room was parked on the floor, he decided to brave the truth to Darby Anderson. "I've never yet met the man," he said. "I've only been in office since January before last, you know, and, usually, my undersheriff handles search and rescues and Remmers."

"I don't much know about all that, except how long you've been sheriff. I'll tell you straight out that I didn't vote for you—too young, too inexperienced. Be that as it may, you're still the Authority Having Jurisdiction in this county, so Nelson Remmers is your problem *as* that AHJ, and I'm filing a complaint. Officially. With you. Right now."

The man handed over a two-page official complaint form, all neatly filled out …by one of the best lawyers in the county, who was also one of the best in the state.

Landon glanced it over, saw words that set off warnings in his brain, and said, "Okay. Hang on, would you?"

Going to his desk, Landon touched on the intercom. "Deputy Somners?"

"Yes, sir?" she answered

"Would you please have someone bring another chair to my office—a nice one?"

"Right away, sir."

Moments later, the chair was walked in by Red. "Where should I put— …Oh."

Red put the chair down, waited for Jessie to get to her feet, then scooted it forward for her. Once she'd sat, Red left, and Landon gratefully dropped into his desk chair.

"All right," he said, pulling out a notepad. "Take it from the top, please."

***

26 – Nelson Remmers

BY THE TIME THE ANDERSONS LEFT, Landon's head was reeling. Bringing up the local website for Nelson Remmers' group, he jotted more notes. Then he called his dad for the lowdown on Nelson Remmers. Hearing an earful in no uncertain language, then asking the requisite 'why's, only to get more of an earful, he thanked his father, said goodbye, hung up, slammed his hat on his head, and headed out.

He took Kins with him, why he wasn't sure. He liked the young deputy, though—somehow trusted him. A fifty-five minute drive later had him pulling into Remmers' run-down, sad excuse for a home kennel operation—nothing nearly as professional as he'd seen on his two trips out to the Anderson place. It was a common thing for property owners to do, though. Keeping it run-down-looking lowered the appraised value and, therefore, the taxes.

The man's dogs went nuts, and Landon felt himself twitch. Kins didn't just twitch, he unsnapped his holster and palmed his can of mace. "Hope that fencing holds them," the young man said.

So did Reid.

"Ho!" a voice bellowed out. Then, "Shuddup!"

The dogs instantly went silent, but stayed at the fence, watching. That really made Landon's neck hairs twitch. It was flat out eerie.

"Sheriff Reid," a short, paunchy, fiftyish man said, walking up all smiles. "What can I do you for?"

Landon wanted to roll his eyes. "Are you Nelson Remmers?"

"I am he," the man said, holding out his hand.

Landon dutifully shook, then got straight to the point. "You know anything about a Jessica Anderson coming out here to see you?"

The man stared at him vacantly. "Can't say that I do," he answered, and Landon swore he was telling it straight.

"She and her granddad?" Reid prompted.

Nelson Remmers frowned, took his hat off and scratched his head, put his hat back on, then went squinty eyed. "...Oooooh. The old geezer in the fancy, white, dually pickup and some young gal? ...Yeah. They came last night. Only stayed a few minutes. It was already past dark, and we were having a training session."

"The meeting you're supposed to hold at the fairgrounds' indoor arena?" Landon asked, prompting again.

The man scuffed his feet. "Well, that. Yeah. Too many looky-loos an' wannabes show up out there. Besides, I have better facilities here."

Landon glanced at the house, then the barn, both with their faded paint, filthy windows, and snow bent metal roofing. "Okay. But it seems they came out to apply, and you sent them on their way rather rudely."

Remmers nodded. Then, "Well, I wouldn't say rudely. Just matter-of-fact. Caught me in the middle of a training session, like I said, and we're not really taking memberships, right now, anyway. Got a good team—all we need. Keeping the crew I've got up on the mark takes a lot of time and work. Plus, a team has to have rapport, y'know. A lot like deputies do." He grinned as he said it. "You know what I mean, Sheriff."

"Mm-hmm. So you're not taking memberships? Then why does your website say that you are?"

"Well, they can apply, for sure. Always looking for good people and all. Most, though, they're not who we're lookin' for. They're just wantin' to be heroes, an' all. But we don't discriminate. Anybody can print out the application and mail it in, along with the fees. Instructions are all right there on the website."

"Five-hundred dollars, non-refundable?"

The man didn't even blink. "We gotta do a background check before anything else. Do that through your office, in fact."

Which doesn't cost you a thing because of your affiliation with my office.

"...And then there's the testin' if the background check comes back okay. This all takes my time and resources, y'know."

"Mm-hmm. Well, I'll tell you what, Mr. Remmers, you waive the fee, I'll give you the pertinent background check information that I have on Ms. Jessica Anderson, and you invite her to your next meeting."

The man shook his head. "I have to test her first, and, like I already said, that takes a lot of my time and resources. I—"

"Then test her, but you do it promptly, and you collect no fees," he said, his voice turning hard, despite his best effort to keep it neutral.

That stopped Remmers dead in his smirk. The man sobered immediately. "Now, listen here, son—"

"Watch yourself, Remmers."

The man's eyes hardened. His mouth set. "Or what?"

"Or I'll pull my office's sanction, that's what."

Remmers' face went slack, then shocked, and he actually stepped back. "You can't do that!"

"Yes, I can. Yes, I will."

The man's eyes got flinty, then calculating, then acquiescent. "Okay, Sheriff. Can we sit down and talk about this, maybe? Missus has coffee on, and all."

"We have been talking, Mr. Remmers. I've told you what you need to do. Now, do it."

"All right. I'll ...do what you say, then." Hands now jammed in his pockets, his arms stiff with tension, he asked, "...Are we good, then?"

"We'll see once you've 'tested' Ms. Jessica Anderson, Mr. Remmers."

"So be it." Then, he squinted at Landon. "...And if she fails?"

"Then, she fails. But I'll be here to watch it," Landon said, his mouth surprising him. He'd had no intention of doing anything of the sort.

Remmers nodded. "I'll call you with the time, then. And I'll get a hold of Miss Anderson as soon as you get me the pertinents."

"Got 'em right here." He turned to Kins. "In my console, you'll find a print out. Get it, and bring my black indelible marker—the fat one."

"Yes, sir."

Kins trotted toward the car. Remmers' dogs instantly exploded, again, and Remmers instantly told them to "shuddup," again. Reid groaned.

When Kins came back with the paperwork and the indelible marker, Reid started sorting through which pages he'd let Remmers have, pulling those he wouldn't and handing them back to Kins. Then, on the remaining three pages, he marked out everything that wasn't pertinent—pages filled with her dog and search-and-rescue certifications. Reid made sure to obliterate the certification I.D. numbers, something that, at least according to his dad, could be used by Remmers for his own benefit. Done, he handed those three marked up pages to Remmers.

"There's no social security number," the man said, looking through them. "And no certification I.D. numbers, either." He looked up squinty-eyed, again. "How do I know this is legit?"

Reid was barely holding onto his temper. "Look at the page headers. What do they indicate?"

Remmers grunted.

"What do they indicate?" Landon repeated.

"That the information comes from the FBI, something called the National Database, and the Justice Department."

"Right. Sent through a secured system directly to my office."

"But it's got no numbers." The man practically whined the words.

"You don't need those," Reid said, "on *anyone*. Driver's License numbers are all you need."

"But—"

"You don't need that information on anyone, Mr. Remmers. Do I have to repeat myself again, or did you get it, this time?"

"I got it," the man said, but he made it very clear that he wasn't happy. Well, neither was Reid.

"One more thing," Reid said. "I want your members list—names, addresses, phone numbers."

Now Remmers face got really sullen. "I'll mail them to you."

"I want them now."

The man blew out a huge breath, stared Reid in the eye a moment, then said, "Okay. I'll go print them out. Take me a few minutes."

"We're not going anywhere."

Reid watched the man drag his feet toward his house. Once he disappeared inside, Kins said, "I don't think he's very happy with us."

"Nope. And I'm not very happy with him. I don't need the legal hassle this guy has potentially instigated. Not only that, he may very well be guilty of fraud and I.D. theft, all felonies, and that's just a start."

"You know he's related to Denny Warsaw, the county commissioner, right?"

"Yep."

"You going to take him on, too?"

"If I have to."

"You're definitely a Reid, that's for sure," Kins said. "You might be even tougher than your dad was. ...Or at least meaner-sounding."

"And you know that how?" Reid asked pointedly, rounding on him.

"He's the one who vouched for me, despite my record as a juvie, and got me into the academy," Kins replied. "He had to really do some convincing of some people to get me in. My dad's a regular in County. ...Jail, I mean."

"I knew what you meant." Reid had forgotten those small details, but he remembered reading Kins' jacket, now. Kins had been caught stealing a candy bar when he was aged six. In Idaho, at that time, that was a felony, though no longer. But they'd been kind and let the kid off with probation and community service. …Six years old. Reid sighed and shook his head. "Right. You were a real bad first grader …and I hope you can see me rolling my eyes, Kins."

"Yes, sir. No, sir. Ah…."

The kid instantly looked flustered. Landon grinned and winked. "Shuddup," he said, mimicking Remmers, and got Kins to laugh.

"Yes, sir."

***

27 – Respect

"*SITZ!*" JESSIE SAID JAUNTILY. Twelve out of thirteen little bottoms plopped themselves down. "*Brave Hunde*," she called, handing out treats. Going to the little one who hadn't responded, she raised his treat just over his head, repeating the command, and he sat to get his nose high enough to reach it, preparing to launch himself upwards, if need be.

Quickly, she gave it to him before he could, stroking with her other hand, and telling him how good he was to '*sitz*'. Then, backing away out of range, she waited until the bunch began to distract themselves before hiss-whistling. They all looked, and, instantly, she called for attention. Then, she asked for the sit, again: "*Sitz*."

This time, all thirteen bottoms hit the floor.

"Brav. Ganz brave Hunde!"

"Jessie, what are you doing?"

"Hang on," she said, giving out the last treats and strokes. "Okay, *geh spielen*. Go play," she said, giving the signal, which, of course they didn't quite recognize, yet. They knew *'geh spielen'*, though, and began gamboling after the basketful of yummy smelling stuffed toys Jessie threw out in front of them.

Turning to her dad, she grinned. "They work better as a group. They learn faster, mimicking each other. They see what gets treats and what they, the ones who didn't quite get it, have to do to get theirs …which is the same thing the others did before them."

"When did you start doing it this way?"

"Back at the humane society in Blaine."

"With young pups?"

"With all ages. Here, I find that working with litters—first just littermates, then with several litters together—seems to give them all a leg up on learning. Plus, I think there's a confidence factor at work. They don't feel singled out or get timid. In a group with dogs they know, they feel confident and not like they're the prey." She paused, realized she was bubbling on about it, and took a breath.

"Go on," her dad urged.

Jessie eyed him. "Well, that's about it. And I don't have anything to back me up, but it's definitely more fun for them, and lots more fun for me, too."

"How long have you been doing this with our dogs?"

"Mmm. Since February or thereabouts."

He frowned, his eyes following the pups as they tussled with one another. "That's why, then," he said, a sudden look of understanding coming over him.

"What's 'why'?"

His attention shifted to her for a moment. "You did this with Lida's litter and Gerta's litter, didn't you," he said, his eyes going far away, again, as, once more, he focused on the pups.

It was Jessie's turn to frown. Suspicious, she said, "Yeah."

"Right."

What's he not telling me? "What's wrong? Are they not proving out? I need to know if this is counterproductive."

He laughed, and, immediately, she felt relief. "Oh, they're proving out, all right, Jessie, my Jessie. They're way ahead in bite training, obstacles, and already starting tactical. Way, way ahead."

Dragging his eyes away from the puppies, he grinned. "As your granddad would say, 'solid gold, Jessica Marie. Solid gold'."

*

"NOPE. ...NOPE. ...Nope. ...Nope."

He couldn't concentrate. The sound was penetrating, persistent, irritating, even with his door closed. Finally, Landon couldn't stand it any longer.

"What is that persistent, rhythmic 'nope' noise?" he demanded, stalking out of his office into the front. Out here, the 'nope's were even more pronounced.

Red Wheeler looked up from where he was going through some paperwork. So did Deputy Ray Hunt who was on rotation manning the desk.

"Well? Can't you hear it?!"

Red tipped his chin toward the smaller of two work rooms. Its door was closed. "That's Kenny Buford going through the photos like you asked him to."

"Oh."

"He's a patient man," Red observed. "This is his second time through them."

"I'd say Kins deserves a medal," Ray put in. "He's having to run the mouse for the guy. Mr. Buford doesn't know how to use a computer."

Landon nodded. Poor Kins. Then, the question that had immediately popped with urgency. "No hits?"

Red eyeballed him. "Nope."

Landon groaned, but quirked a grin just the same at Red's straight-faced cut-up. "Great. Well, I can't get any work done until that stops, so I'm heading out to the Anderson's to pay a visit and try to appease them about their complaint. Call me if we get a 'yep'."

"Yep."

*

JESSIE WAS HELPING DARBY, her dad, and John, who finally had successfully mastered the necessary techniques. Today, they were working the eighteen month and older dogs on their attack strategies. Darby was sending each animal, in turn, at them to do a lunge, grab, disarm, takedown, and hold. This was one of several types of training they did that Jessie abhorred. But, yes, she now knew that, if and when push came to shove, it was absolutely necessary.

Teaching a dog how to safely take an armed man down was imperative if the dog was going to be effective, plus have any chance at all of survival. This was especially true with an amped out methhead or somebody with a knife or gun. The dogs had to learn best how to do it. Acer was alive because he had been so trained. Otherwise, no. He'd have been dead on the pavement back in Blaine, and she probably would have been lying dead next to him along with the people they'd been protecting.

Acer's actions had given her a fighting chance, and he'd only survived because he knew human fighting styles, tendencies, and vulnerabilities. That's what they were training today, and would continue to train until these dogs shipped out to their buyers—how to hit the most vulnerable places and apply the leverage needed to best advantage, while avoiding making themselves vulnerable, as much as possible.

It called for smart dogs—dogs that could quickly analyze human type and temperament, who could adjust their tactics to accommodate situations, and who could calculate effective feints, then hit the most vulnerable target exposed. And, yes, every one of these dogs Darby was sending at her, her dad, and John were smart, canny, quick, and powerful, the big GSDs and the similar but smaller, more agile, and much quicker Belgian Malinois.

It was hot work, because the suits were made of an almost impenetrable material called 'French linen' and heavily padded against the dog's bite penetrating. The pinch of their jaws, though, still would leave nasty bruises, the crushing power of a GSD's jaws something like 238psi or pounds per square inch and a Malinois running at 195psi. Contrast that with the wimpy human bite that weighed in at a measly 86psi. Of course, Mastiffs, Rottweilers, and American Bulldogs had even more powerful crushing power, especially the Mastiff at 552psi, but working with any of them, even inside the protective suits built to withstand it still took its toll. That's why they only did the training every few days—to give her dad, Jessie, and, now, John, time to recover. Having three of them capable, though, made the work go faster with less wear and tear on each of them.

Darby sent one of the big males at Jessica, and, armed with a gun shooting blanks, she aimed and fired, the dog skittering sideways just before she pulled the trigger, then launching himself airborne and nailing her between the wrist and elbow as he hit her full force, knocking her to the ground, the gun loosed from her grip.

Darby called the dog off, then sent a different one at John, who swung at the animal with a club made of a foam covered piece of plastic plumbing pipe. The animal timed it and took him down, the dog's momentum at impact again knocking the weapon loose.

Next came Oli, armed with a rubber knife. A bit trickier, Darby sent a female who feinted, left, then right, caught the right angle and launched herself into Oli, center mass, and, twisting, snapped her jaws around his wrist and wrenched. "Ow!" he bellowed going down, but he hung on to the knife, despite the dog's leverage. He was making it hard for her.

The dog continued to work Oli until, finally, Oli lost the fight and the knife dropped from his hand. Even then, the dog didn't stop until she was sure he'd given up, and Oli still wasn't letting her off easy. Finally, though, Oli raised his arms over his head, turned on his stomach, and covered his head. That was the cue, and Darby hollered the 'out' command of "Aus!"

Instantly, the big sable bitch let go and downed, watching her target.

Darby recalled her, and, with a single glance back, she started to obey. Then, of a sudden, she went over to the knife, picked it up in her mouth, and took it with her back to Darby.

"Oh, *ganz braves Mädchen!"* Jessie cried. "Awesome dog! We're keeping her, for sure. You are *not* selling that dog!"

Darby grinned. "That's Anderson Working Dogs," he crowed, giving the dog's ruff a vigorous rub, then reached into his pocket for a real meat treat for her. "*Guter Hund!"* he repeated over and over.

"I think that's enough for today," Oli called. "I'm now the walking wounded. She managed to get through the suit. Smart, powerful and determined. I'm with Jessie. We keep her."

Jessie laughed. "I think you wore me out, too, for sure, Granddad."

John just was leaned over, breathing hard. He raised a hand and gave a half-hearted wave. Then, he stood up and, taking off his helmet, grinned. "I actually think I'm not getting quite so freaked out. In fact, sometimes, especially with that one big gal, it started to be kind of …maybe fun."

"That's the spirit," Darby said. "So, let's do this again, say, on the overmorrow? Enough time to recover?"

"I want day after the day after tomorrow," Jessie said.

"Day after the overmorrow, then," Darby said, nodding.

John whispered over to her, "What's an 'overmorrow'?"

Jessie grinned. "It's an old time word for the day after tomorrow. As in 'over' and 'tomorrow'."

"Oh. Okay. Got it." Then, "That's a cool word. Going to have to Google® it, maybe start using it."

"Hey, Jessica Marie," Darby called. "I think there's somebody here to see you."

"Oh?" She pulled off her head protection and ran fingers through her sweaty hair, looked toward the barns, but saw no one.

Her granddad jabbed a finger left, and Jessie spied him. It was Sheriff Reid, and, hat in hand, he was staring their way. He was also white in the face. He looked like he'd seen a ghost. What he'd seen, though, was training that few got to witness. "How long has he been there, Granddad?"

"Almost since we started. Thought I'd give him an eyeful and maybe even an education. It pays to earn the respect of them who doubt, but wear the badge," he said, turning toward the man. He said it loud enough that he was sure to be heard.

*

THAT HE WAS INVITED IN surprised him. That he was offered coffee, tea, iced tea, orange juice, lemonade, a soda, or sparkling water doubly surprised him. He accepted coffee and took it black, because he didn't want to push his luck asking for some cream.

"That's some training," Reid said as Jessie brought him in a cup …with cream in it. *How'd she know that?* Then he remembered he'd had coffee when they'd eaten lunch at The Hereford, and the words of her old boss came back—*attention to details*. Around the big living room, the Andersons and some stranger all watched him.

Jessica Anderson dropped to the floor, cross-legged, her dogs parking themselves around her. The act made Reid uncomfortable, but it seemed her preference. Still, his body twitched to get up and stand so that she could sit …except that was stupid, because there were plenty of other chairs around the big room she could use. And he realized that, maybe, she did it on purpose …to *make* him uncomfortable. She'd done it on his first trip out here. She'd done it a few days ago in his office.

Then he thought again. *The dogs!* That was it! She did it to be surrounded by her dogs and wasn't averse to it elsewhere, even without them. *Weird.* As he thought it, all of the animals' eyes shifted to him, and a chill crawled up his arms, then down his back.

"Is checking out our training methods what brings you out here, Sheriff?" Darby asked him.

"No," Landon said. And stuck between what he considered ludicrous and a little bit frightening, he found himself stifling a laugh. The Andersons really had it out for him, it seemed, Darby especially. The man was doing his best to make him squirm, and was somewhat succeeding, to boot, he had to admit.

Landon took a breath and barreled in. "Nelson Remmers has agreed to test Miss Anderson and waived all fees."

"Oh?"

"He's supposed to give you a call."

"Okay. When and where is this all supposed to happen?"

"Should be within the next few days, and I'm going to observe to make sure it not only happens, but that it's fair."

Oli Anderson chuckled, and Reid wondered what was so funny.

"Do you think that you'd know if it was?" Darby asked.

Getting real uncomfortable, now, Reid recognized that he was being scoffed at. Taking a breath, his brain presented the save. "That's why I'm here," he said. "I want you to accompany Miss Anderson and me and make sure it is."

The room grew still. Jessica Anderson's dogs—all seven of them—stood up and stared at him. Getting bolder, he stared back. The big male shepherd—the one Reid really admired—stepped forward, then boldly walked up to him and stood there, real close, watching him. Then, as if having made some judgment—*hopefully a good one*, he prayed—the big animal turned around and padded back over to his mistress and lay down. The rest of the dogs also lay down.

The entire Anderson clan and the young man Reid didn't know seemed riveted by the dog's actions. As soon as the animal had returned to his mistress, all their eyes went to Reid, and those eyes had changed. It was like they had—dare he think it?—a new respect for him, and, to Reid, it felt palpable.

Darby broke the moment. "We can do that," he said. "Thanks for the warning. And thanks for working on this so fast."

His tone of voice has changed. Strange people—sticklers, prickly, and homey, all rolled into one.

Landon got up. "Thanks for bringing the problem to my attention. I've got to get back, so I'll see myself out."

"You passed the test, you know," Oli said quietly.

Reid shifted his eyes to the man. Braving it, he asked, "The dog?"

"Yeah."

Bolder, now: "I take it that's a good thing."

Oli Anderson nodded shortly, a faint smile coming to his thin lips. "Yeah."

***

28 – Pack Test

IT WAS A WHIM—just a whim—but Jessie had seen signs of it during her morning runs, in their group practice, and even in the play yard. Now, she wanted to test the question, and, this morning, the wind was blowing to her favor. To do the test, though, she had to enlist her family and John.

"All day?" her granddad asked.

"Maybe just four hours, but it could take longer. I need to make it hard and real, and the wind is just right this morning."

Darby glanced at her dad. "This will set us back on prepping the dogs we'll be shipping out next week."

Oli nodded, then shook his head. "Jessie helps us training and prepping them, relegating her own business to her spare time. We can do this."

Darby nodded. "It's just the timing."

"I'm sorry," Jessie put in, "but, if I'm right, this might help all of us. I think I've discovered something about pack learning."

Darby frowned and pursed his lips. "Now you've got my curiosity stirred," he said.

"Let's do this," her dad said, and her grandfather nodded. "John?" Oli hollered. "Come help."

"You'll need the ATVs," Jessie warned, and both her dad and her granddad gave her a curious look. She grinned, then explained.

*

AFTER LOCKING UP THE DOGS in her room with chew treats, she gave Darby and her dad time to get themselves 'lost' and well hidden—about twenty minutes, she figured. After they took off, she set up some cameras on tripods, then helped John climb up on top of the barn roof, handing up the video camera. Done, she rechecked the app on her phone to make sure she was receiving signal from her dad and granddad. If she'd had her drones, this would have been a lot easier, but she didn't. So she'd be lucky to catch even a small part of the trial. Still, it should be enough …she hoped.

A text message from her dad and, ten minutes later, a shrill whistle coming though her phone speakers from her granddad, indicated they were ready. Jessie texted back and ran to get her dogs.

"Ready, John?" she called, coming back.

He gave her a wave.

Sitting down, her pals around her, she put down two bags, each containing a dirty sock, one from Darby, one from her dad. She asked them each to sniff, giving the sign for 'two', then 'find', reinforcing that with, *"Such"*—the German—then "Seek" and "Find it."

The dogs watched her. Then, looking about, Queenie began to cast. The others just stood and sniffed air, their heads moving one direction, then another. After awhile, maybe a couple of minutes, the Shepherds and Milo began to cast, too. As they did, Oso and Mitch both sat, put their snouts up as high as possible, and sniffed the air some more. Then, they looked back at her, their eyes questioning.

"*Such*. Seek. Find it," she encouraged.

Both got up to follow the other dogs which were wandering about.

So far, so good. They can't find a trail. Jessica had done that on purpose. She didn't want this easy.

Predictably, the dogs came back to her after about twenty minutes of milling. They sat down, staring at her. "*Such.* Seek. Find it. Find them," she said, giving them the hand signals as well. "Two," she repeated, signing one and one with each hand simultaneously, then touched the scent bags.

The dogs looked at one another. Oso gave a big sigh, stood, then touching a nose to Mitch, gave a little yip.

Jessie held her breath.

Mitch approached Milo, touched noses, then Acer, then all the rest in turn. With a last glance at Jessie, he then trotted off to follow Oso.

Oso headed to the edge of the surrounding woods, stopped, stuck his head up, sniffed, then disappeared. Mitch stopped where Oso had and sat for a moment, also sniffing the air, then turned to the left and headed into the woods in that direction.

Within five minutes, Mitch came back and crossed the field going the opposite way. Again, he disappeared into the woods. Five minutes later, he came back, returned to where he and Oso had both originally started and downed. The rest of the pack just stayed put, watching the whole while.

Twenty minutes later, Oso reappeared. He came bounding out of the woods, stopped suddenly and, bouncing on his front legs, he gave out a series of yips. Mitch raised his snout and barked once.

The pack immediately came alive, bounding toward the two of them. Upon reaching Oso and Mitch, they milled about, Oso touching noses, Mitch, too, and then all of them disappeared, fanning out into the woods, trotting out in slightly different vectors from one another.

"Did you catch that, John?"

"Sure did," he called down. "I can still see them, so I'm still recording."

"Good."

Jessie felt her heart pound. She could barely contain her excitement. She felt tears spring to her eyes. *Oh, my God. What if it's really happening? What if it's true?*

"I've lost them," John said. "I'm turning the camera off till you give me some sign I should start recording again."

"Okay! Thanks."

The wait was excruciating. On her app, she could see the dots of the dogs. She could also see the dots indicating the positions of her dad and granddad. They were only about a half mile distant from one another, but a good mile-and-a-half from the barn and downwind from the dog's starting point. If the dogs could find them without a scent trail, it would be utterly amazing.

Purposely, Jessie had both her dad and granddad ride out most of the way on their ATVs, keeping downwind of the dogs. That meant there was very little air or ground scent until the dogs could stumble upon it or the ATVs. From there it would be easy for them. But, until they found scent or the ATVs, it would be nigh on impossible because the wind was against them. Air scent was blowing the other way.

Something was happening, though. She heard it—yips, but no barks. There was a series of them, and the dots on her phone suddenly started to converge. *What are they doing?*

And then she knew. "Oh, my God." They'd found the ATVs!

The dots arranged themselves, then split into two groups. One dot—Oso's—stayed where they had converged.

Jessie watched one group, specifically Acer, Britta, and Queenie, go one way—toward her dad's position, Queenie leading. The other group—Milo, Mitch, and Sumi, went almost in the opposite direction—toward her granddad's dot—Sumi leading. In moments, each group converged respectively upon her dad's and her granddad's positions. "We've been made," came her dad's voice through the speakers on her phone. It had taken the dogs just over an hour to do the job. "You can come down, John," Jessie called. "They've done it. They'll be coming back with Dad and Granddad."

"Cool! Now, come hold the ladder so I can get down."

"Coming."

*

"THAT WAS THE WEIRDEST THING," Darby said over lunch. "It was like they were on a mission. Had myself up on one of the big boulders out there, and I was watching through my binoculars as they came in, making a beeline for the ATVs. That Elkhound, he was leading, and he just plopped himself down, looking quite pleased

And, Jessie, seeing the dogs work from above, saw things she hadn't guessed at from her vantage point on the ground. There was planning there. There was pack communication. There was strategy. "Oh, my wonder dogs," she whispered. "It's all true. They're doing it."

"I want to know more about this," John said.

"I think we all do," Oli said. "This is a heck of a breakthrough if we can reproduce it with other dogs. Some aspects of training would get a lot easier."

"Solid gold, Jessica Marie," Darby said.

***

29 – The Joke

LANDON WAS WORKING DUSTER on cutting a cow out from its herd when his phone vibrated in his pocket. "Whoa. Let her go," he said, and the horse stopped, the cow making a dash back to the group of milling bovines.

Pulling his phone, he saw the name and shook his head. "You've got to be kidding!" He hit the green icon, though. "Hello." Listened. Said, 'Okay.' Hung up.

"Figures," he muttered, and headed back to the barn. *Always on my day off.*

*

JESSIE TOOK THE WHOLE PACK—all the dogs. She did it on purpose. They took two rigs, Jessie in her Suburban, everybody else except her grandmother, in one of the pickups. "I happen to know Nelson," Ana-Mari said. "I have no intention of subjecting myself to that joker."

John, however, was keen to go. "Wouldn't miss this for anything," he said.

As previously arranged, the sheriff met them at the turn-off to the county road leading to Nelson Remmers' place. He led in.

Remmers came out of his house as they arrived, waved, then stood, hands in pocket, as they parked. Jessie let her dogs out, asked for the sit, then waited as Sheriff Reid spoke with the man. Just like last time, Remmers' dogs barked and howled, only, this time, their attention was on Jessie's dogs. Her dogs ignored them.

Jessie saw Remmers' nod, then glance toward her. He raised his hand and motioned.

Asking for the heel, Jessie approached.

"Which one are you going to test with," Remmers asked her.

"It's a team. Treat the pack like one dog," Jessie answered. She'd prepped herself for questions like this. She was also prepared for what would come next.

But what she expected didn't happen. Remmers just nodded, then said, "Okay. Follow me."

He led them over to a pasture gate beside the barn, beyond which was a field and woods. The back side of the barn—the same barn where he'd held his training session the first time Jessie had been here—opened out onto it. "You've got thirty minutes to find the subject," Remmers said without preamble. "Go to it."

"One subject?"

"Yep."

"Scent?"

"Nope."

A no-scent trial. Just find a human—any human. Hopefully, there weren't any strangers wandering around nearby. Jessie turned to her dogs. "*Sitzen.*" She held up her hands, indicated 'single', 'live', 'human', then released them to search.

The pack simply sat, noses up. Even Queenie just stayed put. Within seconds though, both Oso and Mitch stood. With a glance toward one another, both of them trotted off in almost the same direction, Mitch angling off a little to the left. The rest of the dogs continued to sit, their attention divided between Mitch and Oso.

Mitch angled toward Oso when they neared the woods' edge. Then Oso braced his front legs mid-stride and abruptly stopped. Mitch joined him and immediately sat as Oso lifted his head high, turned toward Jessie and the dogs, and yip-yipped.

Instantly, the rest of the dogs were on their feet and moving, Jessie running to keep up with them. They reached Oso and Mitch, who closed ranks with them, and the lot disappeared into the woods. Jessie plunged through the brush just in time to see her dogs disappear into even deeper cover. Within seconds came alerts—multitudes of barks, then, oddly, howling. A dog appeared—Sumi. She spied Jessie, planted herself into a sit, raised her muzzle and gave two distinctly insistent barks.

Jessie had just about reached her when the dog, assured she was coming, stood, turned, then trotted ahead, turning her head back every few strides to make sure Jessie was following. The other dogs had grown quiet, now.

Busting through the heavy undergrowth, Jessie finally saw them, as, following Sumi, she climbed around an old tractor. There, on the other side, sat her dogs in a circle, their heads turned to look at her.

Mitch stood up and did his stiff-legged bounce, plus a double whine-bark. Approaching, Jessie saw that under his feet lay a circular metal plate, holes drilled in its top. "You're kidding!"

Jessie knelt down, put her eye to one of the holes, then got to her feet, pulled out her cell phone, and called her dad. When he answered, she said, "I need help. No emergency, but I can't secure the search subject by myself."

*

SHE HEARD THEM CALL her name once they got near—her dad, her granddad, John, and even the sheriff. Of course, they couldn't see her, not in the heavy brush.

She sent Milo to fetch them, the big white mutt pushing his way through the heavy undergrowth. A couple of his deep, throaty barks later, and back he came, everybody, except, notably, Remmers, following.

"What's going on?" her dad demanded.

"The search subject is down in there, and I can't lift this," Jessica said, pointing to the heavy circle of rusty metal fitted into the ground, a plate almost three feet wide that looked about an inch-and-a-half thick.

"That has to weigh close to three-hundred pounds," Sheriff Reid said, his astonishment plain.

"Yep," came Remmers' voice. "That's why the tractor's here." He climbed up on the machine, and, after a couple of coughs, the old tractor started with a belch of black smoke.

*

ON HER TRACKING APP, Jessie clocked the pack's find at two minutes-twenty-three seconds. Remmers grudgingly conceded that that was about what he clocked them in at, too, his son down in the hole having marked the time of the dogs finding him on his watch. "We synchronize our watches, and I mark when I tell you to start, and he marks when the dogs finally find him. You passed the test, so I guess you can consider yourself a member of our team, then," Remmers said as they walked back toward his house, the search subject—Remmers' youngest son—walking back with them after his dad fished him out of the hole in the ground. And Remmers was dead serious as he said it.

Jessie considered the whole thing a joke, but went ahead and signed the 'official membership card' Remmers handed her. “Welcome aboard,” he said with a smile that didn’t reach his eyes. “See you at the next meet. But please only bring one of your dogs. Don’t need the whole crew. You can leave your family home, too.”

Stopping in town for lunch, the sheriff inviting himself to join them—The Hereford, as usual—netted Jessie the knowledge that she wasn’t the only one who considered the whole thing laughable.

“Never seen such a farce,” Darby said between bites of steak sandwich.

“Dad warned me Remmers’ system is kind of a joke,” Landon said.

“Kind of?” Oli chuckled.

“Well, he didn’t tell me about the manhole cover, that’s for sure. He did warn me, though, that Remmers is a trickster.”

“How did he wind up leading the county search and rescue, though?” Jessica asked.

The sheriff shook his head. “Dad couldn’t get anybody else consistently willing to do it.” Then he looked slantwise at Jessica’s dad. “And I quote: ‘Including the new folks, name of Anderson’, end quote.”

"I remember that," Oli said, again chuckling. "We didn't then and still don't do SAR dogs, though. That's all Jessie's thing."

"The man and his teams do manage to find people, but, yes, I realize Miss Anderson is way more qualified. Two minutes, and her dogs had him. That's something!"

He turned his face to her. "Do you want to take it over?"

"No. I've got other plans, now."

And all three, Darby, her dad, and John, shifted eyes her way and nodded.

***

30 – Voices

LANDON SCRAPED THE LAST BIT of shaving cream lather off his chin, rinsed his face, then toweled off. "Not bad. No nicks," he muttered, checking the job in the mirror, this, despite the fact that he'd woken up a bit ticked off, which usually meant he came away from the morning ritual looking like his face had met a meat grinder.

He turned the water on in the shower and waited for the hot water. The whole thing had been a waste of time and effort, all of it just to mollify egos. Still, Darby Anderson had pulled the formal complaint. So, it was worth it, after all. But it irked him. "Waste of my time!"

Stepping into the shower, his brain presented him an alternative, though. The dogs—how fast they'd found the target of their search. And they'd done it in a coordinated assault, just like a good S.W.A.T. team. That could be useful—a strategic asset. "Hmmph." She'd said 'no', but he was betting he could change that to a 'maybe', and, then, even to a 'yes'.

His phone jingled just as he was pouring shampoo in his hand. "Of course! First, you wake me up. Then, you disturb my first cup of coffee. Now, my shower. Leave a message," he grumbled.

The phone quit. Then, moments later, it rang again. He stood there, the water pouring on him, the dollop of shampoo cupped in the well of his palm.

It quit again, but instantly went off a third time.

With a sigh, he rinsed his hand off, turned off the water, and got out. Dripping, he picked it up just as it sang out ring number four. It was Daryl Brannigan, county commissioner. "Reid, here. What do you need?"

He listened and squelched an exasperated sigh. The Hogalby Bridge repair was turning into a huge fiasco, and they acted as if he could do something about it. "That would be Roads and Bridges," he said to the man on the other end of the connection, then listened to yet more tirade.

Of course. It was Monday.

*

SHE WAS EXCITED. She had hope. A whole new horizon had just opened up for her. It gave her feet wings. And, of course, she didn't want the work of running an on-call

24/7 county search and rescue group. Let Remmers bungle it. Let the big team out of Boise come. She had way bigger plans, now.

Out since four, Jessie was just coming up on what her granddad called 'Sentry Rock', and she thought of as "The Sentinel', a part of an uplift of basalt that looked like an obelisk that had splintered off and escaped an escarpment of similar rock formations named The Cliffs of Long that lay about a hundred yards northeast of it. The Cliffs were where Lower Long Creek Falls crashed down to form a small lake at its base.

The dogs were already aiming for The Sentinel, more than ready for a rest. She'd pushed it this morning, maybe too much, taking the perimeter trail, though she'd cut off into the woods instead of doing the climb to the top of the cliffs. Even that, though, had added more than a mile onto her usual two-mile run, so she, as much as the dogs, was looking forward to a breather. What she didn't expect when she finally planted her butt on the ground was the dogs to suddenly jump to their feet on full alert, Milo breaking into his all but inaudible deep bass rumble. "*Was ist los?*" she asked softly, rolling to a crouch, instantly on edge.

Acer and Mitch looked around at her. All of the dogs, even Sumi, had their hackles up and rippling, and, suddenly, Jessie felt fear crawl up her arms and neck. She heard voices.

Giving a soft hiss to get all of them to sight her, she signaled the dogs to be silent and started creeping backwards. Quietly, they came, but kept turning their attention back toward whatever they sensed. And, by their attitudes, whatever they sensed was up on the cliffs.

She was about five-hundred yards from the edge of the woods. She had two choices—take it slow and silent or make a run for it. She opted for slow and silent, glad she wore nondescript brown sweats that, if she didn't make any sudden movement, wouldn't be noticeable unless someone was really looking.

Slowly, carefully, her nerves screaming with tension, her muscles threatening to seize, she kept backing until, with relief she realized the trunks of the outermost trees were to either side of her. Seeking even deeper cover, she kept her slow, steady backwards progress until she was deep enough that the treetops occluded her from sight from anyone up on the cliff top.

Crouching there until all the dogs came silently in to stand around her, she waited, breath pent and listening.

Moments later, she heard a scream that sent chills down her spine. One dog woofed softly—Mitch. Again, she hissed and motioned for silence, then for the down. All dogs dropped. 'Still', she signed. And, again, 'silence'.

There was the sound of a car door. Then nothing. Maybe two minutes after that, an engine turned over, revved once, then steadied. Then, the sound faded away. Pulling out her phone, she dialed 9-1-1.

*

LANDON HAD JUST FINISHED dressing for work when the night sergeant, a Will Demers called. "Can't it wait?" Reid snapped. Then, "Sorry. It's just been non-stop since I got out of bed."

"Here, too."

"So, what's up?"

"Ms. Anderson called in a 9-1-1 again a few minutes ago. She's out on a run and heard voices coming from The Cliffs of Long on the upper end of the Anderson property. She said she also heard a scream. She's there, hunkered down in the woods with her dogs. I listened to the recording, and she sounds freaked …er, panicked."

Yeah. I would be, too. "Is she armed?"

"That wasn't asked. I've sent three deputies. One's close."

"Who?"

"Kins lives out there and picked up the call."

"I'm going to head out there myself. I'm around the corner, so to speak, by about ten miles. Send a notice via computer, not the radio, to Kins. I'm on my way. And, Will, I want every available unit heading out there. And call the phone tree for that area. Get the locals to help. Tell them well armed or no go. In that case, they are to shelter-in-place and lock the doors and windows. I want all egress blocked out of there. I don't care if it's a dirt track. You get it covered. I want all vehicles stopped. Let's catch this guy."

"Yes, sir."

"Now, give me Jessie Anderson's phone number."

"I don't know how much service is there. The call was breaking up a lot, but it's 208-610-0474. She's way up on the northeast quadrant of that section."

"Yeah. I know The Cliffs. I'll get there."

Landon tried Jessie's phone. Twice. And got no answer. He tried a third time, and, finally, the girl answered, her voice a whisper. "I'm on my way. So is every deputy in the area, Miss Anderson. Have you told your dad?"

"No, sir. I don't want him alarmed. …He goes …all Navy SEAL, and, well…."

"I understand. We'll be coming in on the old Forest Service road."

"I think that's where they were. On that road. I heard a scream, then an engine start, rev, and fade off."

Yeah, and that road splits and loops around in there. They could be headed right back toward you. "All right. Stay where you are. Are you armed?"

"I've got my dogs with me. They alerted. That's what warned me." Then, "I'm terrified to move out from cover."

"I understand. Stay quiet and still. We'll find you. I repeat, are you armed?"

"No, sir. …Well, bear spray and a bear bomb."

Bear spray! Her answer scared, then angered him. She should know better, especially with a killer on the loose. "I'll be there in no more than fifteen minutes. Stay in cover."

"Yes, sir."

He heard the horrible tremor in her voice, and hated it. This should *not* be happening in his county.

Turning onto the Forest Service road to Long Peak, he flipped his lights and siren on, dodged around the roadblock set up by two of the locals on a call from his sergeant. Both looked like they'd just climbed out of bed. Both had rifles and wore sidearms. Both of their faces were set and hard—determined. He nodded and touched his hat in thanks and respect as he went by and, ramming his foot into it, headed up.

*

JESSIE HEARD THE SIRENS. They were east of her position. Signaling the dogs, she moved, tree to tree, in that direction. The sirens stopped.

Her phone vibrated in her pocket, and she pulled it out, recognized the number as the same as had called earlier, and softly answered.

"I'm nearing your position," came Sheriff Reid's voice. "Another deputy is above me, nearby."

"I'm moving toward you in the forest."

"Good. I'm picking up your GPS coordinates. I'm on foot, headed toward you now."

The connection terminated, and Jessie slipped the phone back in her pocket. She was having a hard time catching her breath. She bent over and worked on trying to stay calm, but it wasn't working. All she felt was panic and terror and guilt and horror, all rolled up into one. Her stomach lurched into her mouth, the acid of it burning.

Mitch and Acer moved near, both dogs flanking her. She heard Milo begin to low growl again. *Oh, God, no. Please.* And, despite her best intentions not to, she dry vomited, her body shuddering. *Stop it. Stop it. Get a grip. Now! Find cover.*

But she couldn't even move. Couldn't force her feet to obey her.

Mitch's nose hit her face. Acer leaned into her, pushing his weight against her knee. Milo woofed softly.

Queenie let out a little whine. They wouldn't do that if there were danger.

From the corner of her eye, she saw Sumi, Oso, and Britta all drop their hackles, but maintain alert. And, moments later, she saw movement—a man in uniform and a white Stetson, an assault rifle in his hands, was walking towards her.

"*Ruhig*," she said, but the dogs already knew—she was safe; they were all safe.

*

SEVEN DOGS IN THE CAR packed the entire back seat—a wall of fur and panting. But, he admitted, they were very well behaved, despite all being sandwiched in side by side like sardines, the two smallest standing on the floor between the seats beneath the others, the biggest keeping his head hunched down to fit.

The girl—*woman*, he reprimanded his brain—was sweating and shivering, both, her sweats sticking to her in places. "I'm going to say this once," he growled. "You do not go out unarmed while we have a killer on the loose. You, of all people, should *know* better. In *fact*, you should know better than to even be *out* knowing that a murderer is using this area for a dumping ground."

"Yes, sir."

He felt steam ready to explode out of him and clamped his mouth shut, doing his level best to lock his rage down. But he couldn't. "You're *law* enforcement. Or *were*. You *know* better!"

"Yes, sir."

He glanced a look at her. Put his eyes back on his driving. "Don't you 'yes, sir' me. That's a cop-out, and you know it. You're paying me lip service, not listening."

"Yes...."

In his periphery, he saw her look away out the window. But he'd already seen it. She was utterly terrified, her skin pale, her lips and fingers blue. *PTSD—was this the result?* May he never, ever suffer it.

The onboard computer bleeped, its artificial voice engaging. 'Unit 24, 10-23. 10-84.' That was Kins. Way too inexperienced for this. "I've got to postpone taking you down," Reid said. "I've got to meet my deputy."

"I know. Another body."

Reid shot another look toward her as he negotiated a curve. Her voice had changed. So had the look on her face. Her color was better, and her shivering had stopped. She was back. Momentarily, anyway.

*

SOMETHING SWITCHED INSIDE JESSICA at the sound of the police codes. Something in her brain snapped, and she felt a calm clarity come over her. She could breathe again.

Her eyes took in location. They were coming up to the property line of her dad's land which crossed about two hundred yards above the falls, maybe a little over a quarter mile from where she'd been just a half an hour ago. A glance right, and there was the tip of The Sentinel. So close. The killers had been *so* close. Had she taken the cliff path, she'd have run right into them. And now she knew there were at least two of them—two different voices that she'd heard.

Sheriff Reid parked. Typed something into his computer—a request for the ME. "I don't know how long I'll be."

"Do you have a PPE pack?" she asked, not quite believing that she was even considering it, much less had said it.

He frowned. "Yeah. In the back."

"And an evidence kit and cameras?"

"Yeah."

"I can help. I'm trained."

She heard him suck in breath. She felt that way, too. What was she doing?!

"You think you're up to it?" he growled.

"Yes."

"All right. Then I'm swearing you in as an emergency deputy. Raise your right hand and repeat after me, 'I do solemnly swear …that I will support the Constitution of the United States, …and the Constitution of the State of Idaho, …and that I will faithfully discharge the duties …of the Bitterroot County Sheriff's Office …according to the best of my ability.'"

Jessie repeated the words—almost the same exact words except for state and county that she had sworn to just a little over a year before.

"Consider yourself sworn," Reid said.

"Yes, sir." *What have I done?!*

***

31 – Shock

KINS WAS SITTING IN HIS UNIT, his face ashen. Reid tapped on the window.

Jerking his head toward the sound, the young deputy's fingers reached for the window switch. "Sorry, sir. Um. She's dead."

"No sorries. And I know. You coded that, remember?"

Kins' hand reached for the door handle.

"No, don't get out. I want you to sit there and, when you're ready, when you're clear-headed and calm, type out your report into the computer. When you're done and have sent it in, then gotten back a response that it's been received, only then are you to drive back to base. Understood?"

"Yes, sir."

"Good man," he said, tapping his palm on the window edge. Taking a breath, he started up toward the crime scene tape Kins had strung up, the plastic ribbon fluttering in the breeze. It was a cold day when this could happen anywhere, much less twice in his county, but here it was.

Behind him, he heard the crunch of feet on gravel. A look back showed Jessica Anderson, her dogs with her, suited up and heading toward him, and, honestly, he didn't know what to think about this turn of destiny. He did know one thing, though. If ever he needed a full-fledged CSI, it was now. He only hoped she was as good as the Blaine county undersheriff had insisted she was.

"I don't think having the dogs here is a good idea," Landon said.

"They'll stay out of the crime scene you've taped off. They're trained to."

Ok-aay. Right. Guess I'm not the boss, then.

Watching her, thinking about what to say back, he saw her move her arms and hands in weird ways and saw the dogs—all of them—range out and begin sniffing the ground. Except the one she called Mitch and the one that looked like a small Husky. They sat down and raised their noses to the air. Then, after a moment, they, too, went off.

What in the world was she having them do? He wanted to ask, but didn't. Instead, he just found a likely rock, parked himself there, and watched her begin her job at the perimeter of what Dave had surrounded with yellow tape. He'd look at the body himself afterwards, he'd decided, watching as she backed up, looked around …frowned. What did she see?

"Queenie," he heard her call, and the red, long-haired setter-like dog came from out of the woods, trotted up to her, then sat herself down in front of her. Moments later, the dog started casting, going slow, back and forth. Suddenly the dog sat again and barked once.

Jessica Anderson moved to her, squatted down, put a marker and a ruler down on the ground, then snapped photos with both cameras.

Landon twitched with the desire to know what the dog had found. He stayed put. Said nothing. One thing he knew, though, it was a darned good thing he hadn't gone to check the body. He'd have walked right through whatever the dog and Jessie were focused on.

Long moments later, after Jessie had finished taking pictures and swabs, the dog moved again—just a few inches. Abruptly it again sat and barked once, then laid down right beside whatever it had targeted, snout pointing downward at it.

Landon was now on his feet. He could barely contain himself, especially when Anderson took out the UV light and turned it on. "Sheriff?" she called moments later.

Finally! Keeping his voice neutral, he asked, "What is it?"

"I think we've got a pretty fresh sample of a human male urinating. I think we just got lucky." She was swabbing like crazy as she said it, sticking the swabs into their tubes.

And, at that moment, one of the dogs in the woods, then two …then a lot, began to bark, then howl. The sound raised instant goosebumps on Landon's flesh.

The girl jammed the tubes into her pack, jumped up, grabbed her gear, and ran, the red dog with her. Alarmed, hand on his holster, Landon chased after them both.

A huge white streak—her monster dog—flew by him, caught up with Jessica, then, dodging in front of her, disappeared into the woods in the direction of the sound. All the animal's hackles, from his neck to his tail, were standing straight up.

Landon felt a black fear rear up inside him. It radiated from his kidneys around to his gut, then upwards, stifling his breath. He slowed to a walk. Unholstered his gun. Then he sprinted.

*

MILO BEAT HER THERE by yards. Then, he, too, sat, raised his snout to the sky, and let out a bone-chilling howl. It was a body—a naked, bloody, male body. Queenie stopped dead and downed. She went no further. Jessie was glad.

"*Brave Hunde*," Jessie whispered, approaching.

Mitch's eyes were filled with sorrow. So were Oso's. Acer, Britta, and Sumi just looked on, their demeanor stoic, resigned, accepting. Milo's eyes met Jessie's, and he came over to her, planting himself in front of her. "*Braver Hund*," she whispered. "I've got to, Milo. I know you're trying to protect me."

The big dog seemed to understand. With a huge sigh, he stepped around her to come up beside her left knee. Behind her, she heard the sheriff stop and suck in a hard breath. As he should. The victim had been staked, mutilated, then gutted, his intestines pulled from his belly.

It had been an ugly, excruciatingly painful way for him to die, and even Jessie wasn't prepared for it. Tiny stars started circling her vision. *I'm going to faint. I can't.*

She squatted, bent her head between her knees, sucking breath, trying to get more blood moving into her brain. It wasn't working, though. The stars got stronger. "Sheriff? I think I'm going t—"

*

HE MANAGED TO CATCH HER before she landed in the middle of the corpse. What he was having problems with was his own visceral reaction. Never in his life had he seen something this terrible except in movies. Never.

He wasn't prepared for it. Nobody could be, except maybe somebody who'd been in a war zone. "Oh, my God in Heaven, help me." And, in that moment, Landon realized that maybe he just wasn't cut out for this job.

Backing up, dragging Jessica's limp body with him, he got himself and her out away from the horror. Her dogs, heads and tails all drooping, followed.

Sitting himself down by the side of the creek, he sucked in the cold wash of air from it. Jessica Anderson held limp against him in one arm, he pulled out his phone, praying he had signal.

He did. Barely.

He didn't call Kins who was probably still parked but a few hundred yards away in his unit. He called Martin. And he was glad for the company of Anderson's dogs which all laid themselves down in a circle around him and their mistress. "Dear God in Heaven, help me."

***

32 – Wonder Dogs

BY THE TIME MARTIN arrived with the ME and the reinforcements he'd brought with him, Jessica Anderson had recovered and was back at work, processing the scene around this fresh body. Landon helped as he could, but he had to keep his eyes elsewhere as much as possible. If she noticed, and she had to, she didn't give any sign of it. For that he was grateful.

Martin Doyle, for his part, also didn't say a word. What he did was take over as incident commander, marshalling the plan of action.

Sidling up to Landon, he asked about Jessica, and Landon gave him a quick rundown. "Okay," Martin said. "She does look like she knows what she's doing in a big way. I've been watching her. But what's with the dogs?"

So Landon explained that, too, as best he could. Right now, he wasn't coordinating his brain with his mouth very well, though.

"Why are there a couple of dogs up on the slope?" Martin asked.

"They're her human remains detection dogs. Miss Anderson thinks there may be more …victims around here. Luckily, so far, anyway, they've not found anything. At least as far as I know."

"Hmmph. Okay. HRD, you say. I'm beginning to like this young woman."

Landon wasn't. It seemed to him that all this trouble had started with Jessica Anderson and her pesky drones. He said as much to Martin.

Martin pulled him aside. "Reid, I know this has shaken the living daylights out of you. I've never seen you this rattled, even after that nasty accident last December. But, God, man. Think about it. If this has been happening right under our noses, isn't it better to find out now before worse happens?"

Reid just cold stared the man. "Worse," he finally said, and he felt like just giving up.

"Yeah. Worse. And don't think it can't get worse."

Landon was, once more, having a difficult time with both his stomach and his breathing. It was like the organs were vying for the same space in his body. "I've got to take a walk."

"You do that. I'll take over helping Miss Anderson."

The sharp deep bark of a dog interrupted Reid's plans, though. Both he and Martin jumped at the sound. Both of them had their hands on their sidearms, Martin wincing and giving up the action that fast, his good arm reaching for his shoulder.

Jessica Anderson came out of the woods, stared up the slope, then, just like the last time, she started running toward her dogs.

Martin and Reid both followed. "God, what now?" Landon snarled. And he wanted to curse the sun and the sky and anything else he could, even God.

*

MILO WAS DOWN, still as a statue. The only thing he did as Jessie ran up was turn his big head toward her. Then he pointed down with his nose.

Kneeling down, Jessica tried to see what Milo knew was there on or in the rocky ground. She saw nothing but rocks and hard ground, though, and she didn't have a trowel with her. She didn't even have a knife.

"It would certainly help to have more than a piece of the hand," Lorenson said.

Getting up, Jessica called Mitch and Milo to her. Signing 'all', 'dead', and 'human', she asked them to cast again, and both dogs went to work, Jessie trailing them. Not fifty yards on, Milo suddenly lay down and gave his single bark alert. "*Guter Hund, braver Hund.* Good dog!" she called, but, inside herself, she felt her spirits crash. Flashes of the other dead corpses blinked in her mind, and she shook her head, trying to erase them.

Mitch alerted—insistently—barking over and over. Opening her eyes, she saw him hop up and down in place, his eyes seeking hers. Beside her, Milo watched her, his eyes worried. She dropped the marker she was still clutching onto his find, gave him strokes, then bent down and hugged the big dog she loved. Taking a breath, then, she straightened, held up her hand, and, when he was ready, asked him to search again, before heading up toward where Mitch was frantically calling her.

"Watch out. Your other dogs are coming at a run," Reid called.

Jessie stopped and looked down the slope. Sure enough, here came her pack. She shouldn't let them, but she couldn't help herself. She needed them. This was too, too much to be alone with.

Reaching her, the dogs circled as she again started climbing toward Mitch. Then something odd happened. Milo came over and parked himself in front of her, making her stop. The other dogs moved in around him, and all of them touched noses with him. Abruptly, Milo turned and trotted up the slope to Mitch, the rest of the dogs close on his tail.

Jessie, Reid coming up beside her, just watched. She didn't move to join them.

Moving in around Mitch, Milo laid down into his sphinx mode, and Mitch started to vocalize, occasionally pointing his head at his 'find'. Then, every dog that had been standing stock still moved in, sniffed, then backed away and, after a moment, trotted off, noses near the ground. As Jessie watched in awe, they spread out across the mountain's long upper face.

"What's happening?" Reid asked, his voice so quiet, but so close to her shoulder that it made her jump.

"I.... I think— Let's just wait and see."

"What do you *think* is happening?"

"I think that the whole pack is now on the search for the dead on this mountain. I don't know how, but, somehow, they've communicated the goal to one another. That's what I *think*. I've got no proof."

Within moments, Jessica had her guess confirmed, though. Britta alerted. Down slope, Acer did, too. Then Queenie. And Sumi. None of them had ever been HRD trained.

One after another, the dogs started giving their alerts, each their own version. Even Oso, mostly an air scent dog. "Oh, my lovely friends," Jessie whispered. "Oh, my wonder dogs."

"That they are, Miss Anderson. That they are."

***

33 – Lumps

"WE'RE GOING TO HAVE to call the state in," Martin said. "We can't handle this alone. There's just too much."

"I tried that already," Reid told him. "They've got their own problems with that war they've got happening. They keep calling *me* for help. A quarter of our force is down there."

"Why?"

"National Guard. They got called up, and I had no choice but to let them go."

Martin shook his head. "You know, they ought to just let the gang bangers and those militia weirdos go at it and kill each other, then round up the survivors and prosecute them to the full extent of the law. That's what I think."

"I know what you think," Landon said dryly. "You and Dad, both. Wholesale slaughter."

Martin blew out a disgusted sigh. "That's what's happening now. To *our* guys."

right?" He grinned saying it. Meant not to. Couldn't help himself.

Jessica Anderson started to chuckle. And then she started to laugh outright, unable to stop. Plopping herself down, she gave herself up to it until what Reid recognized as mild hysteria in both him and her worked its way gone.

Reid squatted down a few feet away and waited. When the fit subsided and she caught her breath, she told him, "You shouldn't do that. I haven't eaten all day, and I think I'm giddy with the horror of all this. I run by the bottom of Lower Long Peak Falls every morning. I almost took the cliff path this morning. I would have run straight into whoever is responsible. This is basically in my back yard, and, honestly, it's freaking me out."

"Yeah. I can understand that." He pulled his pack off, found what he knew was there, and handed it to her—a Snickers® bar.

"Thanks." She took the wrapper off, took a bite and chewed. Then, suddenly, she clapped a hand to her mouth. Her eyes got panicked. "Oh, my God. My family is going to be freaked. What time is it?"

"I had Martin call them and let them know what was up hours ago. No worries on that count, Miss

Anderson." The relief that came over her was keen. Family mattered to her.

"Thank you." Then, she said something that took him off balance. "Would you please call me Jessie or Jessica? I think we're past any formalities at this point."

He thought about it. Wasn't sure, then, deciding, nodded. "Okay. …Jessie."

"Thank you."

"It will be dark soon. You up for doing this again tomorrow?"

"Yes. The dogs and I will be here."

"Good."

*

LANDON DROVE JESSIE and her dogs down to her place, then unexpectedly got invited in to join them for dinner.

"What's goin' on, Sheriff," Darby asked, herding him into the living room. "Sit down. Sit down."

Landon took the same chair he had last time he had been here and let out a long sigh. He was suddenly feeling the long day in every joint and every muscle in his body. "Can't really talk about it, Mr. Anderson."

"Darby," the man said. "Call me Darby. There are way too many Mr. Andersons around here. And we already know about the dead girl. Jessie wasn't under any gag order when you and yours waltzed in here and stole her property."

Reid flinched—couldn't help himself. "Maybe I should get going," he said, getting to his feet.

"Jes' set yourself down. You're a full-grown man. I should be able to talk straight with you. The dinner invitation wasn't a trap, but a genuine gesture of good will. More than you've shown this family, by the by."

Reid shook his head. Darby was direct. He did as bid, but he felt like he was being dressed down by his granddad and didn't like it.

The old man glared at him. "You're using my granddaughter. What danger is there to sit and listen to her old granddad who's a tad bit worried about her traipsin' around up there with a murderer on the loose?"

Again, Reid shook his head. "I've got deputies all over that mountain," he said finally. "Nobody is going to get near her. That I promise."

"Good to know." The old man's face relaxed some. "Jessie is special. I hope you know that," he said, his voice going soft.

"Special?" he asked, thinking the man meant 'damaged' because of the PTSD.

Darby Anderson nodded. "She's the one who will carry this operation forward into the future—our bread and butter and the future of our very special dogs. We can't go having you getting her hurt, maimed, or killed."

Somehow those words made an odd joy flood through him. "I have no intention of allowing anything to happen, Mr. Anderson."

"It's *Darby*, and good, again. So, you going to drop those charges against her?"

Landon frowned. "There are no charges."

"As yet."

"There won't be."

"Also good to hear. What about her property?"

Direct and straight to the point, just like he had a laundry list, and it was Reid who was on the hot seat. "Let me talk to the prosecutor about that. I'll see if we can release it. I can't see keeping it any longer, not with what we now have."

"Good. I don't much care for high-handed confiscation of private property. It's un-American. It's not the way you treat good folk. 'Specially those you owe. You wouldn't even be crawling around that mountain weren't it for Jessie and her search and rescue setup—her dogs *and* those bug-like flying contraptions."

What the old timer said was true, Landon had to admit. If it hadn't been for Jessie discovering that body, they might not have ever known until some hiker or hunter stumbled onto the remains. And they definitely wouldn't have actual leads to finding the monster responsible, never mind being able to find the multiple instances of victims' remains they were now discovering all over Long Peak. "You're right."

"I expect you to do the right thing, then," Darby said. He got up. "Let's pour us a drink on that, shall we?"

Landon laughed and shook his head. "I'm driving."

"Ginger ale do ya, then?"

"Sure."

*

HAVING THE SHERIFF sitting at table with them felt weird, and Jessie was having a hard time with the mixed feelings she was suffering—anger, on one hand, like it was a violation …an invasion of her privacy—but there was also a strange sense of normalcy, as well. Neither made any sense to her, especially the normalcy. There was nothing normal about the circumstances that brought them all to the present moment. Luckily, her dad dominated the conversation, allowing her to just listen.

"I have no idea," Landon Reid answered her dad's question about the road blocks. "There's just no way of knowing when the perp will come out. He's obviously got himself a good hiding spot, though."

"If he's got food and water, he could hole up for a long time," Oli pointed out.

"Yeah."

Her father's eyes flashed instantly a deeper shade of blue. "We're all in danger up here."

"Yeah. I know that. It's why I've got every one of my deputies and my reservists on duty. We're trying to keep everybody as safe as possible."

"You have any idea who did this?"

"Well, as they say, that's privileged information."

"A *cop* out."

Landon laughed. "Double entendre intended, of course."

Her dad nodded curtly. "Of course."

"Actually, it is a cop out. I'm legally bound. But, honestly, we haven't got enough evidence to even begin to narrow down a possible suspect. The guy's smart."

"How do you know it's a guy?"

"Don't for sure. He could be transsexual or a transvestite, I suppose, but, he's reported to be male and the body type on the video your daughter caught of him suggests so."

Oli blew a heavy breath and took a bite of mashed potatoes.

"That's why the road blocks," Landon continued. "We know that the rig he drove in with is still up here."

"He could have hiked out and left the vehicle."

"Yeah. Doubtful, though. There'd be tracks."

"Snow's melting fast, now. Almost gone on the south face."

"It is. But the other reason for my thinking is that he'd probably have been shot. Everybody up here is warned and armed, even Dr. Lorenson's wife," Reid said.

He was speaking of their nearest, practically only, neighbor for miles, and Jessie found Landon's thinking naïve. Most people weren't like her father or even her grandfather. Most people were hesitant to kill or even harm another human being, or even an animal—at least the ones she'd grown up with around here.

"In fact, the only person in the area not armed," Reid continued, directing a stern glance her way, "is your daughter, Mr. Anderson."

Her dad, likewise, directed a glare at her. "I'll remedy that situation."

Then, turning to her, the sheriff laid into her. "Why is it, Ms. Anderson, that you weren't wearing protection this morning?"

She focused on her plate, and refused to rise to his challenge.

"You gonna answer the man, Jessica Marie?" her granddad asked, a certain tinge in his voice telling her he expected an answer.

"Darby," Ana-Mari said softly, and, from the corner of her eye, Jessica saw Darby's hand wave her grandmother off. Jessie was aghast.

"Jessie?"—Darby, again.

Anger reared up in her. How dare he! How dare any of them! "If you'll excuse me," she said, getting up.

She took her plate with her, her dogs leaving, too, their movement eerily silent on the hardwood floor.

*

LANDON SAT THERE completely appalled at himself and Darby—mostly himself. He'd caused this. His mouth had run away with itself. Again.

"That was completely uncalled for, Darby," the Anderson matriarch scolded once Jessica disappeared. "I'm the one who had to treat and bandage her after she took a pistol with her on her morning runs. She developed a deep friction wound more than half an inch deep into the muscle. It was badly infected."

"I didn't know that," Landon heard Darby mutter. The old man had his head dropped and canted away—

shame, Landon knew. He prayed the wife wouldn't push it. The man felt bad enough.

"You don't know a lot that goes on around here. And if you ever dare raise a hand to wave me silent again, you'll be sleeping with your dogs. For good." With that, the woman rose and also started to leave the room. She stopped, turned back, and said, "And you get to do the dishes tonight. Don't come to bed until you're done and the entire kitchen is spick and span."

"Yes, Ma'am."

Landon wanted to crawl under the table. Couldn't. Tried to figure a way to graciously leave. Couldn't. Forced himself to pull his eyes off of his plate, but then couldn't figure out anywhere to put them. Stared at the wall across from him. Then some words came out, again unbidden, his mouth moving for him. "I'm sorry. I didn't know, and I shouldn't have brought it up."

Darby cleared his throat. Sighed. Then said, "Well, at least we know why she was stupid."

"Dad," Oli Anderson chided.

"What?!" Darby demanded, turning to face his son. "You think it's okay that Jessica doesn't tell us when there's a problem so we can all put our heads together to find a fix?"

Oli let out a groan and went for the bowl of mashed potatoes again.

"You know," Landon put in. "There's this new holster they make. It's flat and padded and easy to wear concealed, yet have quick access."

"Yeah. And it hooks to your belt," Darby snapped. "Jessie wears sweats when she runs."

"You didn't let me finish," Landon said softly. "They make a soft strap that goes around your middle that anchors it so it doesn't rub or flop around. I use one when I'm out training. I'll give you the name and number of the manufacturer."

"That might be just the ticket," Oli said. "More?" he asked, holding out the meat platter in one hand and the bowl of potatoes in the other. Landon grabbed the casserole, instead. "I'll definitely have more of this." Then, again his mouth, "And I'll help with those dishes. I'm as guilty as you are, Darby."

"Not hardly, but I'll take you up on it."

"We'll all pitch in and take our lumps together," Oli said with a laugh. "Now have some more meat and potatoes, too, Sheriff."

"Call me Landon."

***

34 – Calling the Cavalry

JESSIE WAS UP BEFORE DAYBREAK as usual, but she didn't dress in sweats, she didn't take her run. When she went out to the kitchen to brew a pot of coffee, she found it already done, her dad sitting at the kitchen table, sipping a cup.

After feeding her dogs, she went back to the kitchen and got a cup for herself, then sat down at the table across from him.

"You're heading up with the dogs, aren't you," he said matter-of-factly.

She nodded.

"I'm coming with you."

She didn't argue. She actually would be glad for his company.

He slid a weapon across the table toward her—a small, semi-automatic handgun in a shoulder holster.

She didn't object. She slipped it on, her dad getting up and coming around the table to help her adjust it.

"Extra ammo," he said, handing her another pouch.

She snapped that to her belt.

"Phone charged?"

She nodded.

"Put this on, too," he said, handing her a small device she recognized as a powerful GPS locator.

"You expect trouble?" she asked.

"Maybe."

Jessica frowned. "You really think the killer is going to show back up?"

"He did, already, is what I know. Don't want to take any chances."

"Right."

His voice was a lot deeper than usual. He was in soldier mode. Jessica recognized it—didn't like it when he got this way. She would have written it off as a 'man thing', if she hadn't seen it happen in women, too. People who'd been in action in the military, male and female, tended to demonstrate exactly this kind of stoic, hard-shelled behavior. They locked down their emotions completely and became war machines. One thing you didn't do when they were like this—especially with her dad—was call them out on it. You went along, and, often as not, nothing ever happened.

Jessie took comfort in that—that nothing ever happened. …Except for when it did.

Memory flashes of that night in Colorado when, out of nowhere and completely unprepared, something *had* happened. Those memories blinked themselves live in her mind just for a moment.

"Jessie?"

She looked up. "Yes, Dad?"

"You back?"

She frowned. "I didn't go anywhere."

"Yes, you did. You've been sitting there staring into space like a zombie for way too long."

"I…." She glanced at the clock, and realized that it was now ten minutes later than she expected it to be. She took a sip of coffee—it was cold. She got up and poured it down the sink, rinsed the cup, and put in on the sideboard. "We need to get going," she said, drying her hands on a paper towel, then methodically throwing it away in the trash can under the sink. And she realized she was moving like an automaton.

"We do," her dad said. He handed her some biscuits with cheese, meat, and egg sandwiched inside. "Breakfast to go," he said. "Get your dogs."

*

5:30 A.M.—just barely daylight. Sunrise wouldn't come for more than another thirty minutes yet. Most of the time, Reid would be just getting out of the shower and heading for his second cup of coffee. Instead, here he was driving around to the roadblocks to check on the status of his deputies and reservists.

There had been no sign of the red truck on any of the roads they'd blocked coming off of Long Peak. Had they missed him? Had he somehow gotten off the mountain before they'd gotten the roads closed down? Or was he still up here somewhere?

Driving to the site, Reid was surprised to see a big Anderson Working Dogs truck parked in what he considered *his* spot. Pulling in behind the big dually, he pulled on a jacket. It was cold—twenty degrees up here on the mountain this morning.

Hiking up to each of his deputies and reservists stationed in strategic positions, he handed each a still hot cup of coffee he'd brought up in insulated totes all the way from town. "Relief will be here soon," he told them. Of course, they already knew that, but it was an excuse to see how each of them was faring—well, he noted. "How long have the Andersons been working?" he asked Deputy Regina Larson.

"Since it started getting light—about half an hour, I guess," she answered. "The man whistles military code. It was odd to hear it. He warned me they were coming up. I haven't heard that since I was an MP stationed in Riyadh."

"Yeah. Oli Anderson is ex-Navy SEAL."

"Wow. Didn't know."

"Yeah. Not many do, I suspect. I do because Dad mentioned it, plus I did a background check on the whole clan."

"How *is* your dad?" she asked, grinning.

"Full of himself."

She laughed. "That's nothing new."

Heading up toward where the two Andersons were, he noted movement up higher on the mountain—dogs working. "Coffee, anyone?" he called, aware that Oli had been watching him the whole time.

Reaching the two of them, he saw Jessie putting shards of something into an evidence bag her father held open for her. "Find anything significant?" he asked, handing them each a cup and taking the last one of two remaining for himself.

"Not really," Jessica answered. "Just more bits and pieces. I think, totaled up, we've got two bodies scattered here, all of it scavenged by wildlife. Can't find sign of the original dump site."

Far above, a dog yipped. Jessie Anderson and her dad both looked up toward the sound. So did Reid. "You stay. Finish your coffee," Jessie said. "I'll go."

Reid watched the young woman climb toward where a big, blonde shepherd stood. He watched her bend down, say something to the dog, then pull out a big evidence bag from one of her pockets. Then came the cameras, the camera flashes bright in the morning gloom. Finally, she reached down, picked up something round and big, then stuck it inside the evidence bag. "Skull number three," she called down.

Reid groaned.

Oli Anderson shook his head.

"We're going to be here all day, again," Reid said.

"All week, you mean."

Reid didn't want to think about it. But he had to. "Guess I'm going to have to listen to Martin and get us some help," he answered.

"I think that's a good idea."

*

CALLING THE FBI, first, which netted him a promise of them being there late the following day, he called for help from surrounding counties, too. That netted him a small team of five skilled people to help collect and catalogue the evidence the dogs found. By the end of day three, they had found a total of seven skulls, some with flesh still on them. Those, in particular, made Reid's stomach do flip flops. He wound up chewing antacids like candy to keep 'the queasies' at bay.

Day Four had the FBI teams there, too—forensic criminologists and a profiling team, to boot. They brought a couple of FEMA HRD teams with them—a man and a woman, each with their own dog. They kept themselves respectful, a Special Agent Andy Newsome acting as a go-between liaison.

Landon immediately felt comfortable around the man. None of them tried to run over the top of him with the usual arrogance and disdain for 'country cops' that his father had encountered the few times he'd called them in. Landon was grateful.

Jessica's father stayed with her the whole week as they worked on covering the south slope of Long Peak using an efficient grid pattern set up by the FBI. The ME, Dr. Lorenson, managed to get a couple of retired doctors, including Jessica's grandmother, plus some forensic experts out of Spokane and from the ISP's Meridian facility to help him, and, with teamwork, they began to be able to sort through what belonged to whom and get a basic timeline.

Frieda Bates had, in fact, been among the victims, dental records confirmed. So had Lily Thompson. Two other missing persons in county records were among the victims, as well, but the identities belonging to three of the skulls remained a mystery. The FBI team sent a rush request on the DNA and dental scans to one of their labs, but got no hits, either.

"Try Canada," Reid suggested, and, sure enough, within a few days, they had an answer for two of the three remaining skulls—Canadians who had disappeared the previous summer. Those Canadians had, supposedly, never left Canada, though. There was no record of them having crossed the border. Canadian RCMP authorities—Mounties—arrived within a day of identifying them. Then, to Landon's surprise, in a gesture of cooperation between countries, the RCMP stayed and pitched in their expertise—all of them forensic pathologists and criminologists. "Could be more of our citizens who are victims," the Canadians said. "We've got at least another four who have disappeared without a trace, some leaving young children." Reid had Barry Olmstead, who was stuck keeping things running in the office, get them booked into the best rooms of their best motel.

"We need to inform the public," Martin said.

Agent Newsome shook his head 'no', but Landon agreed with Martin.

"We need to make sure that folks know that, if somebody, especially a twenty-to-thirty something female doesn't come home on time, to contact us immediately," Martin pressed.

"Oh, that's going to be swell," Barry said. "Put everybody in a panic, and, if somebody happens to stop to pick up something at the store, we've got hysterical phone calls coming in because they're twenty minutes late."

"Better than having more dead bodies," Martin shot back. "Besides, I'm betting most already know what's going down, with all the civilians we've got helping with the roadblocks. Word travels."

They were sitting in Reid's office, poring over the evidence reports. It was nearing nine at night, and Reid was feeling it. So, obviously, was everybody else. But Reid understood Barry's predicament. It was Barry who was saddled with running the day-to-day operations now that half of them were either guarding the roads, doing perimeter duty, or traipsing all over Long Peak trailing after HRD dogs, and what little was left of his force was covering everything all of them usually handled.

"Who are we looking for as a suspect, though? We've got nothing," Barry pursued, frustration edging his voice.

What he said was true. The murdered man, a Stewart Walsh, matched the DNA evidence found on both Sue Bigsby and Debbie Fergus. His thumbs also matched the strangulation thumb marks Lorenson and the ISP lab at Meridian had come up with. Who murdered Walsh, though, was a complete mystery. The only probable potential suspects—Sue Bigsby's father and brothers—all had alibis. The dad and one of the brothers had been at work at the sawmill, and the other one had been getting ready for school.

And there was still no sign of the red truck. The biggest mystery for Landon was why the perp or perps were focused on Long Peak as a dumping ground, and, now, a killing ground, too. "You know, Barry, I want a helicopter. Get one," Landon said.

Yet, again, Barry objected. "We don't—"

Landon rounded on him. "Captain? You know, for a master of organization and bureaucracy, and you *are* that, you always seem to want to throw up obstacles when it comes to spending money. We *will* have a helicopter for this office, if you and I have to go hat-in-hand to every citizen in this county for donations. I want a copter, and I want a pilot. On staff. Too much country in this county to be without one. Should have had one a long time ago. Now, get to it."

"Yes, sir. ...That's going to take time, though."

Landon felt himself deflate as suddenly as he'd gotten up on his high horse. Barry was right. It would. And he needed one now.

His eye caught at the locked metal cabinet where Jessica Anderson's drones were stashed. He turned back to Barry. "You get the paperwork started on getting us a bird and a pilot. Like I said, you're real good at this kind of stuff, so be *real* good this time, and get them as fast as you can."

"Yes, sir. Will do. ...Used bird okay?"

"Yes. And a 'used' pilot is okay, too," he said dryly. "Just make sure he or she is good. I'd prefer retired military."

"Yes, sir."

***

35 – Return of the Drones

"YOU'RE LOSING WEIGHT, Jessica Marie," her gram said, dropping four steaks on the smoking grill.

Jessica reached up and turned the vent fan to high as her gram began to sear them, both sides, then turned the grill down when her gram nodded to.

"I'm going to do scrambled eggs," Jessie said. "How about peppers, onions, and mushrooms mixed in?"

"That sounds good," Ana-Mari said, flipping a steak. "We need to make some hash browns, too. Use the packaged ones in the freezer."

Jessica grabbed a big pack, sticking them in the microwave right in their package. Set the timer and power level, then hit the start button. "Started," she called. She dropped bread into the twelve-slice toaster, but didn't turn it on. That would happen after the eggs were about half done.

"Got the warming oven on?" her gram asked.

"Oops."

"Someone's just turned up our drive," her granddad called.

"Who is it?" Jessica asked.

"Looks like the sheriff, maybe. Or one of his deputies. Think it's the sheriff, though. Got that hat on."

"Grab another steak from the walk-in, Jessica," Ana-Mari said.

"Why?"

Her grandmother rolled her eyes sideways at her.

"Okay."

*

UP WAY BEFORE he had been ready to be, Landon had hit the road at half-past-three. It was pouring rain—miserable weather.

Passing out coffees to the men and woman manning the road blocks from four insulated totes he had in the back, he'd had to double back to get back to the east fork that led to the Anderson place. The difference between the county road and the Anderson drive was like night and day—no potholes. He stuck his foot into it, mindful of the gravel, came around a curve and hit the brakes, barely missing a small herd of cows that bolted. He kept his foot out of it the rest of the way, just hoping he'd make it before they left for the mountain.

"Who has a mile and a half long driveway?" he muttered, pulling in, but he saw that, yes, indeed, the rigs were still there and the lights were on, though it was just four-thirty. Somebody noticed his lights—probably couldn't help but, what with the ruckus the dogs were making. But, then, the Andersons had security cameras, too, so they probably already knew it was him.

Sure enough, as he parked near enough the house so he wouldn't have to tote the gear so far, the door opened and a thankfully unarmed Oli Anderson flipped porch lights on. "Coffee's on," the man said. "My mom's making steak and hash browns for us, if you're interested?"

God, he'd love some. Didn't feel comfortable accepting. "No. I just came to beg some help."

"Mom's already put another steak on the grill for you. Don't insult my mom. She can be formidable, as you know, and she's very skilled with a scalpel," Oli said, grabbing his crotch.

Landon laughed. "Okay. I accept."

"Good. Now, what's up?" Oli asked, and a frown came down. "You've already got our help. What more can we do?"

"I need air power."

Oli looked him askance.

"If you'd come help me juggle this gear," Landon said.

The man didn't even hesitate, despite the downpour. Oli came up beside him, and Landon heard him grunt. Then he turned back toward the house and hollered, "Jessie, come here." Returning his attention to Landon, he said, "Best let her."

"Okay."

When the girl—*woman*—finally arrived, her dogs bounding out around her as usual, she stopped dead, her face blanking, then suddenly going flushed in the glare of the security lights.

That look said it all for Landon. He should have returned them a long time ago. If he'd known then what he knew now about metadata, he wouldn't have taken them, at all, though how and why pieces of tech could be so important to her, he couldn't fathom.

*

JESSIE LISTENED to the sheriff's problem over breakfast. She listened to his idea of a solution. And she thought—out loud—so everyone could hear. "If I take off one of the cameras, I can extend their maximum outgoing flight time by fifty percent. For what you're talking about, we don't need infrared. If we find we need the IR, it's a quick job to reattach those cameras."

"What is their flight time?" Reid asked.

"With all the standard cameras mounted, it's thirty minutes outgoing. If we dismount the IR, that increases to forty-five outgoing, with the roundtrip an hour and a half. We can also extend outgoing flight time if we use a crisscross search pattern, then bring them back on a straight-line trajectory. I've only flown them real time once, though, so I haven't tested any of this. But it works in the simulator, and it's what their spec sheets and manuals say."

"The flight you caught the perp on was their maiden flight?" he asked.

She nodded.

"Sorry."

"Me, too," she said, and saw him blanch. "I don't have a lot of practice using them, is what I mean, Sheriff Reid. I know the rules of authentication and the rules of chain of evidence in law enforcement. You did what you thought you had to."

"Is it doable?" her dad asked quietly.

"Their proximity sensors seemed to work well when they were chasing the red truck. I can program them on a course, put them on semi-auto-pilot and allow them to self-adjust, so, yes, I think so."

"Who will run the dogs, though?" her grandmother asked softly.

"Maybe Dad can," Jessica said, but she was dubious.

The subjects in question were watching, listening, and, Jessie had no doubt, probably catching a sense of quandary in their human's voice—hers.

Her dad shook his head. "Dicey."

"All we can do is try," Jessica responded. "I think they'll work for you. You've been out there with us all week."

"Yeah. Don't I know it. Bones, bones, and more bones, some with remnant bits of gristle," he said, spitting the words out like a bad taste.

"It's not fun for any of us," Ana-Mari said softly. "I'm gaining much more respect for the job forensic pathologists do. And, honestly, I am very glad I chose to heal the living, not learn from the dead."

*

THEY HIT THE MOUNTAINSIDE a half hour later than usual. Luckily, the rain—snow, up here—had quit.

Landon made his rounds. The reports were just the same—no movement except wildlife.

Making his way back around to the south slope, he saw Jessie and her father working on getting her dogs comfortable with him as their handler. To his eye, it looked to be going well. *What do I know?*

Not much.

The crunch of boots….

He turned to see Jessica Anderson coming down between the broken, pillar-like basalt columns that had fallen from the smaller upper falls area of the creek run. "Is everything going all right?" he asked her as she neared.

"They're confused, but trying. We're bonded, so it's tough for them not having me there."

"I bet."

"You know much about dogs?"

He shook his head. "Not a thing. Cat and horse person, here. I do admire the one you call Acer, though. That's some dog."

"All men like Acer, but, all my dogs are something, once you get to know them. If you're not doing anything, I could use your help to plot the search grid. I'm not exactly sure what you want to search for and how."

"Okay. Lead on."

She'd brought her Suburban, a huge, relatively old, and ugly vehicle that was obviously kept in excellent repair. He understood her father's choice, because, yes, he'd checked. The vehicle had been bought for the girl—*woman*, he self-corrected yet again—by Oli before she'd gone off to university. It was a tough, versatile rig, custom-fitted with heavy reinforcements and rollbars.

The man wanted to keep his daughter safe. Reid respected that. He wondered if the girl did.

"Why are you staring at my rig?" she asked.

Startled out of his reverie, he said, "Huh?"

"You're staring."

"Nothing. …I was just thinking that they used to build rigs with full frames like this. Not so much, now."

"You sound like Dad."

Yeah, but no crumple zones, he didn't add.

Opening the back, she pulled some cords out, hooked them to some batteries she had mounted against the third row seat backs, then plugged them into the laptop. Pulling other cords off the cases holding the drones, she laid the cases over and punched in the ID code that released their locks. Popping the case latches, she opened up the lids and there sat the UAVs.

Reid pulled breath. They looked completely alien, like something out of a Sci-Fi movie. He backed away when she tried to hand him one. "Ah…. I might break it. Bull in a china closet, and all, you know."

She laughed. "Just hold it and don't drop it. I promise it won't bite."

Grabbing the other one in one hand, she touched something, and little feet popped down out of the one she was holding. She set it down.

Coming over to him, she took the thing, again touched something to extend its feet, then set it down near the other one.

"Now, for the hard part," she told him.

"Ah, you mind if I call Deputy Kins?"

"Why would I mind?"

"Well.... I don't know. But he flies these things, and he'd die and go to heaven watching."

"Sure."

Reid put in the call to the young man, then said, "He'll be right down."

"He's nearby?"

"Yeah. Just up the road a bit."

"Great."

He saw her glance up the mountain, realized she was checking on her dogs. Opening her laptop, she brought up what looked like a satellite map. "This is here," she said. "When I start the drones' cameras…." She indicated an icon. "…This map will underlay the live-stream feeds, aligning by GPS. What I need from you, though, is where and how you want to search, and what exactly we are searching for?"

"The truck," he said. "It's got to be still up here somewhere, even if the…." He almost said killer, then amended himself. "…Driver isn't."

"Okay. Anything else?"

"Signs of a human roughing it?"

"Okay."

"Can you program all that in?"

"Not really, but I can set up parameters like shapes, movement, colors—in this case, red—things like that."

"Is that inside those machines?" He nodded toward the drones.

She shook her head. "It's in the software analyzing the live-feeds."

"The software on your laptop," he said, frowning.

"Yes. The AI is pretty good, actually, but a lot of it is the operator—in this case, me—catching things as the drones deliver what they're recording."

"Pretty amazing."

"We'll see."

"I'm here," hollered Kins.

Landon looked toward the voice to see Kins jogging toward them. "Kins," he said to Jessie, who'd started. She glanced up the mountain, again. "No!"

Landon turned to look. The dogs were hurtling down the hill, a human—Jessica's father—bounding after them, but lagging farther and farther behind.

"RUHIG!" Jessie yelled. Then some other words in a stream that was complete gibberish to his ears.

Kins stopped dead, seeing the dogs flying down toward them.

Jessica squatted down, holding her arms out toward the coming dogs. She turned her head toward him. "Raise your hands above your head like you're surrendering and turn your back to them. Have Kins do it, too. *Now*. ...Just to be safe. Do *not* draw your weapons. Don't look them in the eye."

He heard the urgency. He did as told, yelling at Kins to mimic him and not go for his gun. "Stay that way until Jessie says different," he called.

"Yes, sir. Done, sir," Kins called back, and Landon saw that the younger man already had.

The muscles in Landon's neck tickled. He felt completely vulnerable, and, worse, terrified.

***

36 – Defense Drive

THEIR HACKLES WERE UP. Even Queenie's and Oso's. Jessie kept up a steady stream of 'doglish'—her mix of English and German. She kept repeating herself, calling for calm, telling them everything was okay. She had to keep her mind calm, her spirit positive, not let her fear for them manifest itself.

Acer, the rest of the shepherds, and Milo flew past her, Mitch with them. Only Queenie came to her. Oso followed the others, stopped, then, deciding, came back to her, too. She rubbed and petted, called the others by name, asking them to come to her, that everything was okay. They were in full defense drive, though. As a pack. They were defending the pack, including her. She recognized that. She also saw her father. *Ignore it. Forget him.*

"*Hier*, Acer, Britta, Sumi. Come, Milo. *Komm*', Mitch."

Acer sniffed around and up and down the sheriff, circling him, watching him. "Acer, *hier*. *Ruhig*," Jessie kept calling, quashing her terror for the dog. Acer dropped his head and turned his eyes to her. His hackles dropped to half. Then, he came.

Then, Milo came, too, Mitch with him.

Relief flooded her. She quelled it. These were the easy ones. They knew the sheriff, had trusted him as safe, already. They didn't know the deputy, though. He was still in danger, so the dogs were in danger—her fault.

She kept calling, but her hands touched Acer, Milo, Mitch—each in turn as they came, rubbing, stroking, their noses touching her face and her responding. And she kept calling for Britta and Sumi. Kept praying.

Britta was watching the man the sheriff called Kins. So was Sumi. Both dogs were intent on something. "What's in your hand, Kins?" Jessica called.

"Mace," came the answer.

"If you drop it, will it go off? Is it like a grenade or bear bomb?"

"No."

Relief. "Okay. Don't move, don't shift positions, don't move your arms. Just slowly open your fingers and drop it," Jessie called, keeping her voice as mellow-sounding as possible, her hands continually stroking the dogs moving in and around her.

Her dogs were still on edge. And they were under stress—confused. They felt a trust betrayed because she'd left them, abandoning them to her father, a man they knew, but who wasn't part of 'their pack'.

She saw the small canister Kins had been holding drop to the ground. She saw Britta nose it, the dog keeping her eyes on the young man as she did it. "Sumi, Britta, *kommen sie*," Jessica called.

With one backward glance, Britta dropped her head and obeyed. She came trotting toward Jessica, her head level, not in obeyance, but attentive.

Sumi didn't obey, though. Instead, she sat, staring up at her mark. But her hackles were dropping, now. She was guarding her capture, instead of intent on taking it down.

Britta approached, stared at Jessica, then, finally, dropped her guard and touched faces with her. "Thank you, Britta. *Guter Hund. Feines Mädchen*," Jessica crooned, rubbing her head, her ruff, her back. The dog licked her face. "Such a good, good girl, Britta."

Acer touched Britta's nose with his, and Britta gave voice to him, tucking her head into his neck.

Standing up, Jessie walked toward Kins, her dogs coming with her, but under her guidance now. She asked them to *fuss*, urging them, then, to stay back, and they did, even Acer.

As she reached the deputy, gently she reached out to Sumi, her dead friend's police dog. "*Hier*," she said. The dog dipped her muzzle, pointing toward the grounded canister. "Okay." Jessie reached and picked it up. "Safe, now," she said to Sumi. Only then did the dog relax her vigilance, downing right there at Jessica's feet. "*Guter Hund, brave Hunde. Ganz feine Hunde*," she said, first to Sumi, then including them all, but squatting down to touch her Sumi.

The dog gave her head to her, and Jessie rubbed hers on the dog, forehead to forehead. Then she stood up. "You can lower your arms, now, Deputy. And, thank you. It's my fault this happened. I abandoned them. Then they saw you coming at me, didn't know you, and they went into full protection, full attack mode."

Kins rolled his eyes at her. "That was scary."

You have no idea how scary, she thought.

"Can I let my arms down, now, too?" Sheriff Reid called.

Jessie turned, grinned, and said, "No. You have to stay that way the rest of the day," surprised at herself that she could sum up even that bit of humor.

He eyeballed her.

"Of course, you can," she said, and he dropped his arms.

Her dad, who'd been standing off, holstered his pistol, and walked up. "You brought them down, Jessie," he said softly. "I thought I was going to have to shoot them. You knew that, didn't you?"

She nodded. "I knew." And she saw realization dawn on the sheriff's face. He dropped his head, then uncharacteristically sank to sit his butt on the tailgate of her rig. Kins came up cautiously and joined Sheriff Reid. Reid said something to him, then eyed her, the dogs, her dad.

Her dad explained it for them. "Packs, once in defense drive, especially when protecting the pack, are all but impossible to stop, except maybe, and that's a big maybe, by the pack leader—Jessica—and, in this case, because Jessie had left the pack, that authority went to Acer."

"The big male," Reid said.

"Yes. ...But they listened to my daughter. They listened." Her dad let out a sigh, his eyes flicking to hers. "It's why we don't use packs, but rather keep it to one dog, one handler. ...But." And, here, Jessica saw real admiration come into his eyes as he glanced her way. "Jessie's bunch just proved that, even in full defense drive, her pack will listen to her. Our mistake was separating them from their chosen leader—Jessie." Then, specifically to her, he said, "Won't be doing that, again, will we, Jessica!" It was a statement, not a question.

Jessie shook her head. "No, I won't. Never again."

***

37 – Drone Master

"HOW GOOD ARE YOU at flying drones?" Jessica asked Kins, once she'd given the dogs some dehydrated beef strips to chew on, then asked Sheriff Reid to properly introduce them.

The young man shrugged. Jessie saw Reid drop his head, an exasperated look on his face.

Jessie understood, then. She eyed the lanky deputy. *No bragging, so expert. But probably with a controller, not software.* "I use the software to fly them, programming in my search pattern and using the auto-pilot and self-correction capabilities, but there's also a controller," she prompted. "How to control two at once with the controllers eludes me, though."

Flustered, Kins eyes sought anywhere else to be, but kept returning to stare at her drones.

"What are you thinking, Miss Anderson?" Reid asked.

"That, since he's a deputy and since he at least has an amateur drone license from the FAA, that he can fly them if you're willing to fudge the regulations a little. Then, I can get back to work with my dogs finding remains." She glanced toward her pack as she said it, and they were all still busy working on the dried strips of beef she'd given them. Acer noticed her look, though, as did Milo and Mitch. They started to rise. The others paused and then began rising, too. "It's okay. *Sie essen.*"

They watched her, then, almost simultaneously, all of them relaxed, lay back down, and went on chewing their meat strips.

"Can I try the simulator first?" Kins asked, his voice hushed.

"Sure."

Logging back into her laptop, which had gone on standby, Jessie brought up the app.

"Can I use the controller?"

Jessie laughed. "They're still in the cases." Popping open one of the cases, she pulled one out. It was still in its shipping wrapper. "Here."

Kins stripped off the packing, stuffing the shredded wad into his pocket.

"Give it here," Reid said.

Kins grinned sheepishly, pulled it back out and handed it over. Reid slipped it into *his* pocket, and Jessie just wanted to laugh at their silliness.

Slipping in the battery pack, Kins stood back, watched the screen, and began to play in the simulator. Both Reid and Jessie watched, intrigued as Kins proceeded to run through the beginner level, switched to intermediate, then hopped onto advanced, ripping through the exercises and obstacle tests like they were child's play. *Okay. Definitely expert.* "Let's try it with the drone," Jessie suggested.

Kins' eyes shifted to hers, then dropped to the drones. He took a noticeable breath. "Okay," he said tentatively, and, with an adeptness that Jessie envied, he switched the remote to live.

The lights on the drone on the right blinked on. The little machine made a beep—ready. Then it unfolded, Reid stepping back, his eyes going wide and a frown crossing his brow, as the machine extended its arms and rotors. "Looks like an alien *bug*," he muttered, stepping even farther away as the machine lifted and began to hover. "A great big flying cockroach."

"Cockroaches are brown. These are light blue-gray," Jessie said, and got rewarded with a snotty glare and a roll-eye.

Getting a drone airborne was one of the tricky things because of ground effect. Kins got the little machine airborne without a problem, though. Then, even with the stiff breeze coming off Long Peak, he hovered the craft, first at about eight feet, then descending to about five. Next, he spun it on its vertical axis. "What are you doing?" Jessica asked.

"Testing my control of it, its aerodynamics and control sensitivity, plus my ability to safely fly it."

Jessica laughed. "I'd say you're both getting along just fine. I think it's a nick," she said turning to Sheriff Reid.

He let out a big breath as if he'd been holding it. Didn't respond.

"What's a 'nick'," Kins asked, never taking his eyes off the controller's little display. He was now flying the drone in a circle just above their heads.

"A very good match," Jessie answered.

"Oh. …Thanks. This is an awesome unit! Real responsive."

"Glad you like it. Let's see if you can handle the software. It's too obvious you're a master at flying with the controller."

The man blushed. "Thanks," he mumbled.

She turned to the sheriff still standing by watching them. "I think you and Deputy Kins here will be able to run the drones, and I can get back to working my dogs, if that works for you?"

Reid nodded. "If you trust us with those contraptions."

She grinned. "You break 'em, you buy 'em," she quipped, and saw him grin.

He touched the brim edge of his hat with two fingers. "Done."

"Actually, they're insured," she said with a smile to let him know he was off the hook.

He shook his head, though. "We'd still compensate you for any damage. You're not the only one with insurance."

*

THEY'D BEEN AT IT for two hours before, while trading drones, Kins got the idea to run at nearly ground level. "Why would you want to do that?" Landon asked. "Seems dangerous."

"If I overlay the topographical maps she's got with the satellite maps, then overlay the drone feed, running each overlay at about a third opacity, I can find the trails, then maybe follow them at about human eye level. May see broken foliage, recent wheel ruts, maybe even garbage. Haven't seen a red truck from above, that's for sure, so maybe he covered it in brush to hide it."

"Okay. You're the joystick jockey, here. I'm just along for the ride."

For Landon, watching the drone feeds from above was okay. Watching things zoom by like he was flying in a mini-airplane was dizzying. He'd played video games as a teen …still did sometimes, but this was more like driving way, way too fast through heavy brush. Dave Kins didn't seem bothered by it, but Reid felt like they were going to crash any second, and that crash would hurt. He kept jerking and flinching. A glint. "What was that?!" he yelped.

"What?"

"Back up, rewind ...whatever."

The view tipped up, the sky appearing, spinning, swirling, then dove back down to swing back to a normal orientation. "Wish you'd quit that. I never signed up for fighter pilot training."

That comment got a snort of laughter out of Dave. "So what am I looking for?"

"I don't know. It was a silver glint— There!"

Dave stopped abruptly, and Landon felt like he should feel the momentum, but of course, that was just his brain acting weird. "Okay. Um... maybe ease back a few feet, if that's possible.

Again a blur, this time like a horizontal spin, and Reid's stomach felt it. The view steadied, then crept forward.

"I see it!" Dave said, whispering suddenly.

The field of view shifted downward. "What *is* that?" Reid demanded.

"I don't know. I'm going to increase magnification." The on-screen view blurred in and out, adjusting, then cleared. "Oh, good. The AI just figured out what we are targeting and auto-focused," Dave told him. "Let's go closer down."

Descending, then twisting the view around finally brought some sense. It was a jumbled pile of canisters—black caps with a mostly white rectangle with 'RUST-' visible.

"Rust-oleum® paint cans—flat black color," Landon said. "That's what we're looking at. He painted the truck black."

"It would look horrible. Anybody would know it was a hurry-up hand paint job and be suspicious," Dave said.

"Yeah. But a black truck parked in the shadows would be really hard to spot, *especially* flat black. That's why we can't find it."

"Are there tire tracks?"

Both Dave and Landon jumped at Jessie's voice. They hadn't known she was there. Her father was with her. "You always sneak up on people like that?" Landon asked. "You do know we're armed, right?"

She smiled. "Jumpy, huh? It's lunch time. Aren't you hungry? Dad and I certainly are, and the dogs could use some water and a snack, too," she said walking off, the creatures mentioned all moving along calmly around her. The contrast between the animals that had all but attacked him and Dave this morning and these was startling.

Landon glanced at his watch. It was half past one. They'd been at it for hours, with nothing much but bad news to show for it. "Let's make a run to town, Dave," he said. "I think we could both use a bite."

Oli Anderson walked up toting a red cooler. He popped it open and handed Jessie a plastic container. "No need. We've got extra," he said handing Dave a thermos and a bottle of water, then offering the same to Reid. "Hot, homemade soup."

Jessie handed both of them two sandwiches each, and then two small brown bags.

"We always pack extra just in case," Oli Anderson said. "Eat up. There's pop in the blue cooler in the bed of my truck, too. Don't mess with the green one. That's not jerky. …Well, it is, but it's for the dogs."

"Cookies!" Dave said, opening the brown bag.

"You eat your real food first, kid," Oli said. "You're skin and bones, mostly. Need some meat on you, so you need to eat some."

Kins' eyes shifted sideways and his face flushed. He unwrapped a sandwich and took a bite. "Wow. Real roast beef!" and began to chew in earnest.

Jessica smiled, watching him. So did her dad.

***

38 – Tracks

"DID YOU SEE ANY EVIDENCE of tire tracks?" Jessie asked between bites of her own sandwich, repeating the question she'd asked earlier. She wanted an answer, and they just weren't cooperating. *Probably because I'm just a woman.*

Still, nobody answered.

Pressing on, she said, "It's been days. I'm guessing they're long gone off the mountain, and, since they've been doing this over a period of at least a couple of years, I'm guessing they're using the old skid trails and cat tracks for ingress and egress. I would."

The sheriff nodded, swallowed, then said, "Only hitting this road once the old trails run out up here where it's never been logged. I was wondering that, too, but there's nowhere to go that doesn't wind up on a county road, sooner or later."

"What about the old trapper cabins?" Oli put in. "Or the remnant buildings of old homesteads? We've got two on our property, alone."

Nobody said anything. There were so many possibilities.

"Wish there was a way to spot tire tracks easy. Like blood evidence that glows in UV," Dave said.

"There is," Jessie said. "Broken flora. And most people will use the same path repeatedly once they find connecting trails that work. That's why I keep asking if you've seen evidence of tire tracks."

"Oh, you mean tire *ruts*," Reid said.

Different strokes. Communication breakdown. Jessie groaned. "Yeah. Continuous parallel tracks in the landscape. The undercarriage of a vehicle will break over small trees and bushes, the exhaust system will scorch vegetation, and the tires will crush whatever they roll over."

Reid gave her a look like she'd called him an imbecile. *Well, stop acting like one!* "It's something pretty easy to spot from high up," Jessie offered, mollifying her tone.

Reid looked at Dave. Sighed. "Okay. After lunch, we go back up high and start looking all over again."

"I'd program for three to four hundred feet. No higher because that breaks into aircraft territory," Jessie advised. She did not need her drones confiscated again, this time by the 'altitude police'.

Dave laughed. "Got in trouble once about that when I was fifteen. Luckily, they just gave me a lecture and a rule book. Told me I had to register with the FAA and get a license."

"How high did you get?" Jessie asked, excited to know, and saw her dad's eyes go 'tired'. Tech stuff bored him to distraction unless it was *his* tech stuff …like flying planes and helicopters.

"I'd passed the 10,000-foot mark. I was so excited. I got video of traffic looking like tiny ants, of real trains looking like models, of airplanes taking off, a helicopter landing…. It was *so-ooo extra*. …Then the cops came." He grinned. "I still have the video."

*

"YOU THINK THE PAINT CANS were a diversion," Kins asked once Landon came back from cancelling the roadblocks. The young deputy already had a drone in the air, using the on-screen controls to fly it instead of the controller.

"Why would you think that?"

"Well, like I said, hand spray-painting a vehicle would definitely make it stick out. What if he left those spray cans in plain sight to just make us think he painted it a different color?"

Landon turned on his heel and headed back for his rig.

"Where are you going?" Kins yelped.

"To rescind my last order cancelling the roadblocks."

Thankful that his previous order hadn't yet been executed, Reid wound up spending an hour on the phone dealing with the Hogalby problem again with one of the commissioners. Done, he answered a call of nature, then headed back to where Kins was still glued to the laptop, and found Jessie and her dad back down off the mountain, the dogs all sitting and lying quietly around them as they stepped up to watch the laptop screen, too. "What's up?" he asked.

"We need to talk …once you've heard what Deputy Kins has to say," Oli said.

Landon switched his attention to Kins. "Speak up."

The kid flushed, instantly flustered.

Must be hereditary, or something.

"The deputy who collected the cans didn't see any tracks, and she said the ground was pretty soft," Kins told him.

"She still there?"

"Come and gone."

"You spied on her?"

"I helped her locate them," Kins said, looking for all the world as if he'd just been reprimanded.

Landon ignored it. Kins was going to have to toughen up and not take things so personally. "You can speak through those machines?"

"No. I used my phone and then led her in with a drone."

"Actually, those are two-way microphones on them, but using them uses more battery power," Jessie Anderson put in.

"Right."

"Thing is, she didn't see any tracks or impressions," Kins repeated, "and that's soft ground."

"Then I'm glad I still have those roadblocks up."

"I don't think they'll catch anything," Jessie said softly.

He threw daggers at her. "What?!"

"I've been watching as Kins does the sweeps. There's another road ...well, more of a really faint skid trail. But I think, by how noticeable it was, that it's had vehicle traffic lately."

"Where?!" Kins asked.

"Why didn't you say something?" Landon demanded.

The woman sighed. "Because I'm not sure. I wanted to see if it held on each sweep."

"Show us," Landon said, checking his temper into the tightest lockdown he could. *This is what her old boss meant—you gotta ask the right questions. She doesn't volunteer anything!*

Using a mouse she plugged in, she tagged something and an inset appeared, playing a part earlier in the recording as Kins continued to follow the track he was already on. Landon realized with a start that the machine that he'd had locked up in his office for weeks was something very powerful and very special if it could do what she was doing with it while Kins continued to do what he was doing. *Amazing.*

Then he actually saw what she pointed to, her fingers tracing a looping pattern through parts of the recording. It hadn't been clear at first, but, with her pointing it out to him, he could definitely see what she was talking about. "Well, I'll be. Good eyes."

Kins spoke up, never taking his attention off what he was doing, "Should I abort this search?"

"I think so," Landon said.

"Where to?"

Jessie showed him, pointing to a place just west and down slope of where the first body had been found, then crossing back and forth across the forest service road until it disappeared into even heavier timber. Landon could clearly see it, now that she'd pointed it out. *That's her training as a CSI, her being able to pick that out that way.*

Kins maneuvered the drone upslope and dove down between the trees. Landon's brain objected, his eyes begging to close. He kept them locked on the feed, anyway. *Why didn't we see that when we found Sue's body?*

Starting his run, Kins sped down the track—and it was, in fact, a track. "It looks like it continues down the west slope of Long Peak," Agent Newsome said, peering over Landon's shoulder.

Landon turned. He hadn't realized the man had joined them. "So, then, we *do* cancel the road blocks, now. Where does the trail end?" Reid felt excitement rising in him.

"I can't tell, yet," Kins answered.

"There are a lot of small places on that side," Oli observed.

"Yeah. I know."

The Anderson girl was staring at him as if she was waiting for something. "Something you need?" Landon asked.

"I want to engage hyperspectral cameras—actually FLS cameras, to be accurate, but they include hyperspectral imaging. Once you're done with my drones on this job, that is."

"What kind of cameras?"

"Hyperspectral imaging. Originally developed to identify mineral deposits, they can 'see' bones," Jessica said. "It'll speed things up, because everybody's tired."

"We are," Newsome put in. "If she's got the equipment to do it, it will make it go faster."

"I have the cameras, but haven't mounted them. But I can, now that I've got the drones back." She paused, watched him, then said, "Again, though, you'd need to secure a search warrant to do it. And I want to extend the search to the west slope of Long Peak, too, since the vehicle tracks seem to head across it."

The warrant wasn't a problem. At all. What troubled him was her extension of the search field to Long Peak's west slope. "You think there's more bod— …Bones?"

Her eyes dropped. Agent Newsome didn't say a word. Neither were a good sign. Jessie spoke first. "I don't know. I hope not," she said, raising her eyes to his. "But I'd like Kins to do the flying, so we can just go to an area the cameras identify and start working. The imaging can show us what's above ground—the high probability areas—but it will take the dogs to find the hidden stuff."

His brain went into its blurred whir. "Won't it pick up animal bones, too, though," his mouth spit out without telling him beforehand. As usual.

"Yes. But I'm hoping for skulls, hips, that sort of thing—things that are obviously human."

"We'd miss some bones though, right?"

"We would," Newsome put in. "At this juncture, though, I think we're far ahead of what we would have ever recovered without Miss Jessica Anderson's dogs—some of the best HRD work I've seen."

Landon shook his head, not wanting to. *So we'd miss some, but not that many, is what they're saying, and going over every inch of this mountain, never mind the adjoining ones, would take months.*

Landon sucked in a big breath, held it, decided, then said, "Okay. Let's do that. I'll get Barry started on the warrant. Should have it within the hour, I'm guessing. …Deputy Kins?"

"Yes, sir?"

Landon turned to look at him, expecting the man to be attending him. He wasn't, though. His eyes were on the screen, the live-feed showing the drone still running down a track between the trunks of trees, the branches whizzing by. Landon shook his head. He had his answer. Kins would do it. The federal government was helping pay the overtime, so the county commissioners would be off his back.

***

39 – Frustration

"WE'LL NEED GPS COORDINATES every time the cameras show a hit," Jessie said, showing Kins how to send via the computer to Newsome's phone app that she'd shared. "Agent Newsome said he'll coordinate locations to dog teams."

"That's smart," Kins said, grinning. "These are just amazing machines and more amazing software!"

Marking out what she knew they'd already covered, Jessica guided the drone over an area high up on the south slope that none of them had yet searched.

Kins let out a yelp. "It's a skull! Looking right at us!"

"Where?" Jessie didn't see it. That upset her. She was trained to.

"Go back!"

Back-tracking, she slowed the drone. She didn't have the skill Kins had to manually fly it and watch the feed. Frustrated, she asked, "Take over?"

"Sure." He slid his fingers onto the big touch pad and, that quick, got the drone to swing back. "There," he said. "Isn't that a skull?"

Yes, it was. And, around it, traces of the rest of the skeleton embedded in what looked like rock, but Jessie guessed was actually hardened soil. She'd missed it completely. "Coordinates?"

Kins tapped the icon with his little finger, never losing control with the ones he was using on the pad to maneuver the drone. Jessie envied his skill. "We're going to head over there," she said.

"Okay. I'll figure out a search pattern and, when I see something, I'll send you the numbers, Agent Newsome."

"The guy must have at least seven brains to be able to multi-task like that," Jessie told her dad as they headed up. "I think he's in the wrong career."

Oli laughed. "Yeah. You should know about that."

Jessie shook her head and looked away. "Don't start, please, Dad."

"Then don't waste yourself on fruitless pursuits, Jessie. You're a natural dog trainer—I'm betting the best in the world."

She felt her face flush.

*

JESSIE'S CAMERAS SHOWED multiple bodies, some obviously still partially intact and obviously human. "We're going to have to search the rest of Long Peak," she told them. "The West slope, and even the north face. Maybe the adjoining mountains, too."

"I agree," Agent Newsome said.

Landon stared at the two of them—his FBI liaison and 'the dog girl'. "That will take weeks …months!"

"Probably," Newsome said. "…I've got more help coming," Agent Newsome put in after too long of an uncomfortable silence. "Two more forensic teams and some six more HRD teams from FEMA. I've also put in a call to the universities if this goes into summer, which it looks like it will. This is too big for any of us, now. Way, way too big. A possible nineteen bodies, so far, going back at least ten years, maybe more."

Landon felt himself go cold. *Ten years….*

*

"Okay."

*

"HOW CAN THIS BE?!" Landon bellowed, the deputies surrounding him—the ones going off swing shift and the ones coming on graveyard—all looking down at their boots or their hands or the floor, anywhere but where they should be.

He knew he'd lost it. He knew his ugly temper had finally escaped his iron grip. He didn't care—not at the moment. All the dead. And in his county!

But not all on your watch, came his mind's unbidden thought.

Who cares?! At least six of them were, he shot back to it, and that quelled his ever-churning brain.

Behind him, he heard rustling. He ignored it. "We've got nineteen bodies, now, and maybe bits and pieces of others," he said, modifying his voice and his desire to yell it out. "These are your kith, your kin—your friends and relatives, children of your friends and relatives. How can this have been happening without somebody, *anybody*, having even so much as a clue?!"

Nobody answered.

More rustling.

Holding up a closed hand, he extended his index finger and bent it back with the other. "We've got somebody who actually sold the truck to our suspected perp. *Saw* him. *Met* him." He extended his middle finger and bent it back. "We've got video imagery of him." Now, he extended his ring finger and did the same, "And we've got a darned good idea of how he's gaining access without using the main roads. We should be closing *in* on this guy. *Heck,* we should have him locked *up* by now. But we've got *nothing*. Just more and more bones piling up!"

Agent Newsome cleared his throat. "Sheriff?"

Landon rounded on him and saw the whole team of profilers standing in the doorway watching him. "What?!"

"Serial killers like this evade law enforcement because they are so rare and appear, in everyday life, so normal. Nobody expects it. Nobody anticipates it. Sociopathic killers aren't average criminals, and your deputies …even most FBI agents, we're trained to deal with criminals and their crimes, not psychos parading as Joe or Jane Normal-Everyday-Citizen."

"Your team," Landon snapped, thrusting his chin at the five standing there.

Newsome nodded. "My team and teams like us, yes, but we're specialists. We train for years. I repeat: serial killers—most of them, anyway—seem like *normal*, everyday people. You'd never suspect them. *Never*. Don't blame your deputies. Don't blame anyone. Not even the unsub. He's sick, damaged …can't control his urges. But he's also smart and very skilled …crafty and knowledgeable. Time to get back to work, and let your deputies get on with the jobs they've proven very dedicated and very good at doing."

Dropping his head, Landon suddenly felt ashamed. He'd deserved that dressing down. More, even. *So* deserved it. …*So, own it*, he told himself. …*To the good men and women standing here having suffered your stupidity and unjust criticism.*

He looked up, looked at each of his deputies in that room, swallowed, then said, "I apologize. You didn't deserve that. …I was wrong. It's…. Just chock it up to my stupidity and frustration."

Eyes raised. They watched him.

"I don't expect your understanding. I won't let it happen ...*ever* again. ...I'm just ...sorry," he said, the last coming out almost as a whisper. And he hoped they knew he meant every word.

Retreating to his office, he went in and closed the door, locked it, turned off the lights, then just sat staring out the window, his eyes on the Bitterroots, on the mountains that he loved.

***

40 – A Teaching Moment

SHERIFF REID WASN'T HAPPY with her. Agent Newsome and the RCMP experts were on her side, though, and that helped. Having a day off from clambering around the mountain did the dogs a world of good, as it did her and her dad. Being home was like an elixir, breathing new vitality into her, her dad, her pack.

Numa, the bomb dog—her dad's choice—wasn't picking up on it, though. Frustrated, Jessie tried again and again, using the real human remains she'd begged off the FEMA teams.

"This isn't going to work, Jessie," her dad said.

Plopping down in the tanbark, Jessie just wanted to cry. It should work. It *should*.

Mitch and Milo. They'd 'talked' to the rest of the pack—their pack. But would they 'talk' to Numa? "Let me try one more thing," Jessie said to her dad who had joined her on the ground, the nine-year-old Malinois female lying down next to him and watching them both.

The dog was panting. Her eyes were dilated. She knew somehow that she wasn't pleasing her humans, and that made Jessie sad. "*Guter Hund*," she crooned. "*Sehr gut*. It's our fault, not yours, Numa."

The dog nosed her dad, and he wrapped his arm around her. "Okay. One more thing. Only. She can't handle much more stress."

"I know."

Getting Mitch and Milo, Jessie introduced them to each other—no problem. Then, dropping target articles, she asked the dogs to come and pointed to them, telling them to 'find it'.

Mitch and Milo looked at her, tails tentatively wagging in confusion. This was baby stuff, they were telling her. Numa sniffed, her eyes confused.

Jessie moved to the next. "Numa, *such*."

Moving from one to the next, all around the working area, she begged and pleaded, Mitch and Milo trailing along as Jessie repeatedly asked Numa to alert to it.

Mitch sat suddenly and whine-barked.

Jessie looked at him. "What? *Was ist?*" she asked.

He got up and trotted up to her. Sat. Lifted a paw.

"I don't understand."

"I think I do," her dad said. "Let Numa loose and leave them alone. Come over and sit with me and just let them all alone."

Doing as bid, Jessie unleashed Numa. Immediately the dog downed. Jessie signed for Mitch and Milo to stay, then backed away, turned and went over to where her dad still sat on the ground. Sat down next to him. "Now what?" she asked.

"I don't know. Let's just be still."

Minutes passed. The dogs just lay there. Then, all at once, Mitch reached his nose over to Numa. Sat up. Stood up.

Milo got up. Started moving from scent item to scent item. Mitch followed him, pausing to look back at Numa, then at Jessie, then at Numa, again.

Now the bomb dog got up. She looked back at Oli, then turned her attention back to Mitch and Milo. Hesitating, she took a tentative step towards them where they stood as if waiting. Looked back at Oli.

Then, all at once, as if deciding, she trotted over to Mitch and Milo. Put her nose down. Lifted her head.

Mitch nosed her. Whined a little.

Milo moved to the next item. Stopped. Waited.

Mitch followed moments later, and, after another small pause, Numa joined them.

So it went. When Milo began again at the first item, Jessie caught on. "They're teaching her," she whispered, and saw her dad nod just ever so slightly, then indicate silence.

*

AGENT NEWSOME'S TEAM noticed it. "Did you know that there were no law enforcement personnel included in the pictures shown to Kenny Buford? There are no state, city, or sheriff's personnel included, at all," Agent Newsome said. "None."

Reid looked a question at the man. He was sitting with them, and so was Martin. They were going over everything they had. "I didn't order that," Reid said.

"I think it's the new default setting," Martin said. "That new software the state has forced on us. I think I remember seeing that there's a checkbox on the bottom, already checked. It leaves out law enforcement personnel."

"You're right," a woman named Special Agent Lynn Corelli said. "But there are also no men included who have anything but dark brown or black hair, either. Or anyone with anything but blue eyes."

"That's the description Kenny gave us," Reid said. "...Which matches what we have on video recording."

"Hair dye? Wigs? Contacts? Remember, this guy's smart. Knowledgeable. Methodical. What we call organized. He knows how to avoid detection—no skin oils, no skin flakes, no hair." This came from a man named Special Agent Justin Holt, a man who reminded Landon of his first year dorm-mate at ISU—smart, confident, quick. *And intimidating.* Landon was still friends with him—a lawyer now, doing what Landon had wanted to.

"What about the urine Jessica Anderson found?" Martin asked.

"That belonged to the murdered man, Stewart Walsh."

"First I've heard about it," Martin said, and Landon nodded. Him, too.

"I'm sorry. We must have neglected to include that in our daily briefing."

Landon shook his head. "Not necessarily. I probably wouldn't remember even if you had. The whole thing is too huge."

"We've made a new set of possibles. We've had the images manipulated to compensate for hair and eye color, and we'd like to bring Mr. Kenny Buford back in to look through them," Special Agent Corelli said.

"Do it."

"How many individuals," Martin asked.

"We've narrowed it to just over two-thousand, based on our best analysis. That's better than the eight-thousand we started with, though."

Landon groaned. "Poor Kenny. I suppose I'm in there."

"Actually, no."

"I'm the right size and in the age range."

The agents, all of them, exchanged glances. "You don't fit our profile," Agent Corelli said finally.

Landon eyed her.

"What she means is you don't have the necessary propensities," Holt said.

Landon stared at him. Saw the glint in his eye. "You mean I'm not smart enough."

"Not in our unsub's way. You're not cold-blooded, either."

Martin began laughing. Clapped Landon on the shoulder. "In other words, Landon, you're too dumb and wimpy to pull this off."

***

41 – Before Color

NUMA HAD GOTTEN IT. Within an hour. She was a happy, happy dog. "You know this means I'm going to have to treat her like *my* dog until this is over," Oli said to Jessie over a quiet breakfast at the kitchen table. It was three-thirty in the morning, and the rest of the house was still sound asleep, but she and her dad had both felt it, both gotten up, practically running into each other in the hallway. There was a tension in the air.

The brindled Malinois sat next to him, owning him as hers. And he was owning her, too. Her jaws snapped as he dropped bits of his breakfast off his plate for her, and Jessie smiled. "You used to have a dog," she said softly.

Her dad's head dipped. "Yeah. …She died."

"I know. Wasn't she a Malinois, too?"

"Yeah."

"What's the problem?"

He raised his head, eyes shifting from his plate to the dog. "They die too young."

Jessie understood that problem. But Malinois often lived longer than GSDs. She said as much. "She could have another four to six years, Dad."

"Maybe."

"Wouldn't you rather have a friend for a few years, rather than no friend at all?"

Her dad picked up the sausage sitting uneaten on his plate and flipped it, spinning, into the air. Numa immediately launched herself to snap it up, mid-spin, at the top of its arc. "Time to get going, Jessica. I want to be up on that unholy mountain way before he can see color."

"Okay."

*

JESSICA AND HER DAD were back on the mountain working. They were, as yet, the only ones up there. The mountain being the last of his rounds, he was happy to see them there. Then he saw the new dog. She eyed him as he approached, immediately planting herself in front of Oli and staring at him. "Am I going to get bitten?" he asked, never pausing his climb.

The man said something to the animal, and it sat. Its eyes never left Landon's, though. "That a 300 Win Mag?" he asked, eyeing the rifle Oli Anderson had slung on himself, military style.

"It is."

Landon nodded. "Coffee?"

"Thanks."

He went down to where Jessie worked and offered one to her. "A new dog?" he asked, tipping his head up toward her father.

"She's Dad's. We spent yesterday …well, Mitch and Milo did, teaching her to search out human remains."

"That quick?"

"She's Malinois," Jessie said, grinning. Then, "But she's a trained bomb detection dog, so it was a matter of transitioning her to HRD."

"Oh. And that can be done in a day?"

"Not usually."

He nodded. They weren't sharing. Something had changed. "Well, I've got to get back to town."

"Okay."

Landon nodded. He was still in shock. Barry. *Can't be.* His own captain. But his own records, checked and double checked by the FBI, had pretty much locked in that Barry had absolutely no schedule conflicts that gave him a solid alibi for the times of the latest killings.

"His car's not at his residence, either," Martin said, walking in. "Red's there with a team. Neighbors haven't seen him since Sunday last. Say he only shows up about once a week to cut the grass. Told them he's living with a girlfriend."

"His unit?"

"Still here in the yard."

"Where is he, then?"

"He have any family we don't know about?" Corelli asked.

"No immediate," Landon said. "All dead. Most of his nearest relatives are all in Oklahoma."

"That's what we tracked down. And he doesn't seem to have any friends we can find."

"That's not right. I know he has kin. He mentioned them," Martin said.

Landon called his dad …got told to talk to Sam. "He knows everything and everyone," his dad said.

*

"YOU KNOW, I SEEM TO REMEMBER something about his gram …or maybe great gram. Not sure on that. Let me go visit a friend," Sam Hull said.

"May I come with you?" Landon asked. Newsome nudged him. "And Agent Newsome, here?"

"Sure …if you don't mind visiting an old folk's home."

Landon shook his head and chuckled. Obviously, Sam didn't know that he visited theirs regularly …or did before *this* nightmare started. "I don't mind." He turned to Newsome. "You?"

"Not at all."

*

THE WOMAN, A SELMA THAYER, was ancient. "You remember old Gabby Lyn Roberts?" Sam asked her after about ten minutes of catching up chit chat.

"Of course I do."

"Isn't she related to the Olmsteads?"

"No. Only Olmstead I know of was Roberta, and she married *into* the Roberts family. Came out of Oklahoma. She's was an in-law, not a blood relation. Big difference, there. Gabby's son Harold married her while he was stationed over there."

"Okay. I remember. It's Roberta. She was Barry's aunt," Sam said, nodding.

"You mean Barry Olmstead? Yeah, she was. Took care of him ...all those three kids the summer their mom died. I think that's probably why Barry moved back here. Fond memories of that summer, and all. Sad little boy, as I remember. But Roberta died young, too. Too bad. She was a nice girl."

"What happened to Harold's place?"

"Still in the family. It's a part of one of those family trust things. All the Roberts property is."

"So who would live there?"

"Probably Gabby's great granddaughter, Flora. Gabby, she was the matriarch of that family, y'know. She had a thing for Flora, and that was a real nice house and property. Off the beaten track, and all, but Flora liked that. She liked things quiet."

The old lady's face scrunched up, then cleared. "Flora must be in her late thirties or forties, now. She makes art for some company back East. There was a write-up in the paper a couple years past about her doing it . Cutesy stuff and all."

"You know her married name, by chance?"

"She never married. She's still Flora Roberts, as far as I know. And I read the paper every day, so I'd know if she went and got married or died, even if I wasn't invited to the wedding or funeral ...which wouldn't happen."

So, Flora Roberts....

"Let's go drive out there," Sam said, once they said their goodbyes, then got the address from the Assessor's Office. The property's location was at the end of the county road that ended where Minnow Creek came down between the west slope of Long Peak and Green Hump. Looking at the satellite images, it had about a hundred-yard-long driveway that ended in a broad apron in front of the house and a detached one car garage. The whole of it was set back in the trees, good for them, but good for Barry, too, if that's where he was holed up.

"We'll need backup."

"We'll need your S.W.A.T. team," Newsome said, his phone already at his ear.

***

42 – Lock and Load

THEY CAME IN ALL STEALTH MODE—the S.W.A.T. team leading.

S.W.A.T. went in on foot, moving from tree to tree. They needn't have bothered. Nobody was there.

The garage was empty. One of the S.W.A.T. team members found Flora's car. It was sitting in the woods, covered in pine needles and dirt. Out in the unused barn behind the house, they found the truck parked in the central alley. It *had* been spray painted black, and it was missing the two front grill teeth. It also had the deep gouge in the back bumper. Landon took out his pocket knife, scraped a nick of paint off where it wouldn't be that noticeable. "Sure enough. Red."

Inside the house, the FBI agents and some of his deputies were doing a search. They found Flora's checkbook, a bank statement, and a file cabinet filled with up-to-date paid bills. But there was no sign of Flora.

Landon wondered if Flora was the girlfriend Barry had mentioned to his neighbors. They were about the same age, her a bit older, but not looking it.

Landon was still having a hard time believing that the man his dad had trusted, the man he himself had been working next to for his entire career in law enforcement, from rookie deputy to sheriff, was the killer.

Agent Holt came out from the laundry room. "Hamper's full of men's clothes," he said. "No women's, at all. Not even undergarments. Does Flora wear men's clothing?"

"I have no idea," Landon replied. He knew some women did.

"Look here." Sam came out of the bedroom holding a deputy uniform in a plastic bag, its dry cleaning tag still hooked to the neck of the hanger. "The tag reads 'B. Olmstead'," he said.

Newsome emerged from the bathroom. He was holding an evidence bag. "I don't know any woman who shaves their whiskers, and the shaver—a man's shaver—had a few whiskers stuck under the head."

"Color?" Holt asked.

"Looks blond to me. Could be light brown."

Flora had dark brown hair. Barry was blond. "So where's Barry?" Landon asked.

Newsome answered with a shrug. "Obviously, not here, right now. I say we put the uniform back. Put everything back, and get out of sight. Be*fore* he comes back."

"If he hasn't been watching us the whole time," Landon said.

"That's what I'm thinking," Holt agreed.

"He could actually be out looking at a helicopter," Corelli said.

"I'm wondering where Flora Roberts is,"—Newsome.

Landon wondered that, too. He didn't like thinking about it.

*

JESSIE AND HER DAD, plus one other HRD dog team, were pretty much alone on the south slope. Upslope, two forensic teams were working on some difficult extractions, one a Canadian team of two, the other an FBI team of three. Everybody else was over on the west slope where Kins had seen evidence of human bones with her drones. A couple of deputies were down at their cars. The rest had disappeared.

Jessie was searching out the last of the lower slope grids while her dad and his dog worked the upper. The other team was working the middle where there were also some remaining unsearched grids. They knew they had at least the rest of today and tomorrow to go before joining the others on the west slope.

Searching out the last of the creek bed one more time, Jessie saw no end in sight to the long, tedious job. Her body ached, especially her back, hips, knees, ankles, and feet—mostly her ankles and feet. Clambering for hours in the rock strewn terrain which had an average slope of anywhere from thirty to fifty degrees was wearing on her after nearly two weeks of it. All of them felt it—Jessie, her dad, and her dogs. Numa was the only one of them bounding and bouncing.

The team of Canadian forensic specialists working nearest was about a half mile up from her. Their site comprised the buried portions of what was suspected to be a single individual—the one whose skull Kins had spied. The other team of three was working way higher up, pulling bits and pieces of a mystery victim found close by.

The one thing all of the forensic techs were happy with was the number of bones recovered—even tiny ones—and all because of a dog's scenting ability. Using a pack had proved much more productive than using just a few dogs to do such a huge job, but Jessie was glad for the help of the FBI's HRD teams. Without them, they'd be out here beyond tolerance. *Beyond forever*, Jessica thought. She missed working with the pups. She missed her daily routines. What *ever* had made her think that she'd want to spend her life looking for the lost, strayed, or dead. Now, she knew better. Once more, her dad and her granddad's advice—ignored—had proven true. Search, rescue, and recovery was not as fulfilling—not nearly—as training dogs was for her.

Alone with her thoughts, she watched her tired pals keep working. Dedicated to her, and, admittedly, she to them, this would be the last time she ever asked them to work this hard. They were tired. They were losing condition, despite triple rations of fat and meat, plus the booster shots Dr. Kathy Caldwell had given them.

"Never again," she promised them, handing out chunks of, not dog jerky now, but real raw beef as they all took a break for a snack and water.

*

LANDON PULLED EVERYBODY in he could. He got the State Police to help. He warned Dispatch not to communicate via either computer or radio. Phone only, one on one, until they had their target.

The safest course was to catch him on the road, but Landon was taking no chances. "We're setting up a trap at the house, too."

They reconnoitered the property, then brought in ATVs in case Barry made a break for the woods, stationing themselves around Flora Roberts' house, camouflaging themselves with debris from the forest, glad for the cover the trees provided. S.W.A.T. dug in nearest the house and garage.

Then they waited. …And waited. Landon was sitting parked in his unit between two trees, his nice, clean vehicle now covered in last fall's tamarack needles and dirt to hide it. He wondered if Barry had split town already.

An hour passed, then another.

Movement. On the driveway.

Two figures. Walking.

Where'd he leave his car?

Watching, his nerves making his eye twitch, Landon held his breath. He prayed nobody would cough or step on a branch.

It was Barry. Landon saw the man. Next to him, a younger man—skinny, with long, black hair—chattered on about something Landon couldn't make out through his open windows.

He heard Barry answer. Were it up to him, they'd take him out on sight—one well-placed bullet to the brain stem. But, of course, that didn't sit well with policy or the courts. The rule was to try to take them alive, never mind the danger to law enforcement.

Let S.W.A.T. handle it, he willed. Those were the rules. Those were his very own orders. But some of his regular deputies were hotshots. *Let S.W.A.T. handle it.* He blew a silent breath, every muscle screaming …and waited for S.W.A.T. to make their move.

*

IT BECAME A HOSTAGE SITUATION in less than three seconds. Landon saw it happen. What he didn't anticipate—none of them did—was that Barry, who only ever barely passed his yearly firearms requalification tests was, in fact, deadly with a gun.

He had two men down, the boy with him held like a shield in front of him, before disappearing into the house. Within moments, S.W.A.T. had that house surrounded. Landon and the rest of the force emerged from hiding.

Agent Fuller, the member of the FBI team skilled in hostage negotiation, went to work with a bullhorn. Nobody answered him.

More gunfire erupted, radio chatter now telling them that Barry and his hostage had fled out back. "Officer down!" came the call. "Officer down!"

Landon rammed it in gear and, driving through the bushes that lined the side yard between the house and the garage, busted through the back fence. He was vaguely aware of S.W.A.T. team members running alongside, using his rig as cover.

He almost managed to end it right there. Instead, he missed by inches. So did S.W.A.T.

Chasing after, Landon tore up the wooded hill behind the barn. The man was on one of his department's ATVs, the deputy who'd been riding it bouncing like a limp doll, head lolling, against his back, Barry using her like a shield. Landon felt sick. More, he felt rage.

Behind him, three other ATVs were closing. They outflanked him, taking shortcuts through the brush. He aimed for where he knew the trail wound around and up the mountain. It was the only way up for his four-wheeler. He just hoped he'd get there before Barry if his deputies didn't take the man out first. "Pray they do."

He floored it, bouncing and yawing and spinning up the trail through the forest across the lower west slope of Long Peak, heading for the south one.

*

JESSIE HEARD THE SOUND of an ATV. They were coming to collect more of her evidence bags. Calling the dogs, she waved and headed toward her cache. Then she saw arms flailing, jerking—extra arms.

Above her, she heard her dad yell. She turned to look. He frantically waved, signaling 'find cover'. He had his rifle in his hand.

Ducking into the tumble of angular boulders fallen from the upper falls cliff, she heard the sound of more

ATVs. ...Gunshots—small arms fire. From above, the boom of a large caliber rifle. *Dad.*

She heard the crash—metal rolling, bouncing. She cowered against the rock, the dogs pressing near.

Silence.

Where's the rider? Hurt? Dead? It's got to be the perp. Why would he come back knowing we were up here?!

She pulled her sidearm, flipped the safety off. She had to think.

More shots fired. They ricocheted off the rocks to the north of her. Close. Spraying chips. She ducked down and scrambled away, the dogs with her. She had to find a better hiding place. She had to think.

She figured she had three choices, to find a good spot to try to get a bead on him, to find a better place to hide, or to let him take her hostage and depend on her dogs, her dad, or one of the deputies to take him out.

The first would be tough in the cover she had, hiding was her preferred choice, but letting him take her hostage was the best chance for survival for both her and the dogs if her dad and the deputies realized what she was doing.

But she'd already run. The man knew she knew he was whom law enforcement was chasing. He probably knew she had a gun. No dice on that, then.

She was running out of time and options. She could hear him—the noise of his movement, the soles of his shoes scrambling on rock. *He's west of me. Maybe fifty yards.* Pulling herself in between two boulders, she dug out her phone, blessing the autofill and the AI that knew how she texted. 'L Falls rocks. Will break for cover downhill. Perp closing.' Then she added, 'Don't shoot my dogs.' She sent it out to group 1—her family—and to group 5. That group was 9-1-1 and Sheriff Reid's phone number.

Crouching, she sucked breath, preparing. Hissing, now, she caught the dog's eyes, signaling '*platz*' and '*bleib*'—down and stay. Repeated it. "I don't want you coming with me. *Stay*." Then firmly, "*Bleib*."

More deep breaths.

With one last glance at her dogs to make sure they were doing as told, she made a dash for it, heard a shot ring out—large caliber, again.

*

THE MESSAGE CAME, vocalized through his speakers in the computer's ever calm voice, and Landon felt his stomach drop. Ramming his foot into it, he tore up the last remaining yards of ground, aiming for the lowest of the rocks that stood between him and open ground.

He took it at an angle, praying he wouldn't overturn. The rig bucked, scraping hard on the rocks, tires spinning, grabbing, throwing the rig sideways in lurching jerks. "Come ON!" It bucked, then found traction, ground over the top. Barry was but about fifty yards from him.

He saw her dash out from cover, aiming for the trees. He saw Barry aim. She turned. Fired. Barry fired. Then the man jerked—hard. Something had hit him from behind. Blood spurted from his shoulder.

Jessie was down and rolling. Back up on her feet and running. Barry'd missed. He was wounded. But he was drawing aim again.

His foot jamming the throttle into the floorboard, Landon begged the machine to get there, aiming purposely for the ridge of angled rock that Barry stood on. How he wished he had a machine gun mounted on the hood.

In front of him, something brown hurdled through the air, a bigger body hurdling with it—the dogs Mitch and Acer. And then something even bigger—white—Milo. Barry went down, the dogs on top of him, tearing at him.

…There was no way he could stop, now. "Get out of the way, you lunks!" His hand on the horn, his brain frantically praying, his rig hit and went airborne just the way he needed, as if by Providence. "Thank you," he said, mourning that he was destroying a darned good vehicle even as he said it and braced for impact …then saw Barry manage, despite torn face, neck, and chest, to roll upright. He saw the gun raise—just a glimpse, but it froze there in his eyes, Barry looking square at him, his weapon trained. "This is it, then." But in that blink, as muzzle fire flashed from the weapon, the man's head exploded. Landon's windshield took the hit as he felt his rig connect.

***

43 – Dead and Alive

JESSIE WATCHED IN HORROR as Acer, Milo, and Mitch scrambled to leap clear of the hurtling vehicle, the perp's head dissolving in a blast of blood as the sheriff's unit crashed right into him, then flipped completely over, nose first, the shooter's body disappearing under it. "Oh, my God!"

The engine stopped, the dust settling. She smelled hot radiator fluid, then gas. Then she saw her dogs. They were alive. Acer limped.

She picked herself up, and, ignoring the pain that shot through her knee and leg, ran toward the overturned vehicle.

*

SURPRISED HE COULD, Landon heard the hiss. Surprised he was alive, he smelled the gas. Upside down, his head jammed against the headliner, one of the roll bars was pressed against his neck. Fumbling, he tried to hit the release on his safety harness ...failed.

He couldn't see. The deflated airbag blocked his vision. So did his hat crushed down on his forehead and over his eyes.

He tried to find his pocket and the knife he always kept there—couldn't do it. Couldn't squeeze his hand under the restraining belt.

"*Landon?!*"—Jessica Anderson's voice.

"I hope you have a knife. Cut the belts."

About then, he felt himself loosed. She already had.

*

HE WAS HEAVY, curled wrong. The smell of gas was strong—acrid—the fumes burning her eyes. She heard something that sounded like a gas furnace igniting from its pilot light. Black smoke boiled. Crackling. The rig was on fire. She had to get him out.

She felt Acer come next to her, then big Milo, too. *Where's Mitch?*

Landon's head popped out, his arms reaching, pulling. His shoulders caught.

Acer and Milo both grabbed a piece of the man's shirt as she desperately tried to extricate him, a man whose shoulders were too big to easily fit through the bent and twisted window frame.

Then, suddenly, they all went tumbling as he somehow propelled himself into them. "Run!" he yelled, scrambling to his feet, the dogs bounding sideways to get out of his way.

Jessie felt him grab her, lift her by an arm, her shoulder popping. He dragged her along, her hip and legs bouncing against rocks, the dogs scuttling along with her.

She managed to get her feet under her …almost, then did.

*

HE KNEW IT A SPLIT SECOND before it happened. "GET DOWN!" he yelled.

She didn't. She was screaming something. To the dogs, he realized.

Slamming into her, he knew he hurt her, as he dropped on top of her, covering his head and neck with his arms. In that moment, he saw two dogs leap to disappear into the forest. He hoped they all had made it. "Dear God in Heaven, protect us."

The concussion felt like a sledge hammer hitting him, the sound deafening him instantly as heat and pressure blew the secondary gas tank, the one that hadn't ruptured. He felt as if his soul had somehow shaken loose of his body, but the feeling vanished moments later, and he was real again.

Debris—hot, searing, burning—raining down, the chatter of it all around him. The stink of burning wool—his uniform—the stink of burning human flesh—maybe his own, maybe Barry's—he didn't know. He couldn't feel anything at all. …Black, acrid smoke.

Everything was silent, except for a vague ringing that was coming from inside of his head. *My ears. I can't hear.* Then, slowly, the sound of crackling getting louder …louder. "Thank you, God."

Easing himself off of the still body beneath him, he touched her shoulder. "Jessie?" God, he hoped he hadn't hurt her too bad.

She groaned. Then, her hand reached out to press the rocks beside her head. "My dogs! Are my dogs okay?!"

He looked around. Didn't see them through the smoke. He'd heard her call them enough. Should know their names by now, he told himself. …Tried to remember. Then his mouth moved. "Acer? Mitch? Milo?" he called, though, to him, his voice sounded far, far away and so, so muffled. He managed to remember them all. "Britta …Sumi …Oso …Queenie," he called.

Jessica managed to roll herself over, then, using his belt as leverage, sat up. Vaguely, he heard her begin to call them, too.

From out of the trees they came—Mitch, then Milo, and, finally, limping badly, Acer. Then the others, the red one bounding toward her, the fuzzy, small Husky one, too. …The other shepherds.

*

FROM OUT OF THE FOREST and over the rocks they came bounding and limping toward her—her Acer, her Milo, her Mitch. Then, from the opposite direction, through the smoke, here came her Queenie, her Oso, her Sumi, her Britta. "*Kommen*, come," she called, catching at them with her one hand—the one that worked—as they converged on her. "Oh, my wonder dogs. My wonder dogs. Oh, my God. Thank you. Are we all okay? *Brave Hunde. Brav.* Good, good, good, good, *great* dogs." She buried her head in their fur—each one. "I love you."

"Are they all right?"

Sniffling, never realizing till that moment that she was weeping, she turned to look up at his worried, filthy face, and threw her head back and laughed. "We're alive—all of us. That's all that counts. Thank you for coming to our rescue, Sheriff Reid."

*

"IT'S LANDON," he told her as her dad, his dog with him, came lunging across the rocky berm, stopped upon seeing his daughter, and, heaving, squatted down and bowed his head, his dog staring down at them.

Landon watched Oli Anderson for a moment, then glanced at Jessica. "It wasn't me, you know. You can thank your dogs and your sharpshooter dad for saving our bacon." Then, "Oli Anderson? Thank you."

The man glanced at him, a disgusted look on his face. "Took me four rounds," he grumbled between gasps.

"At over a thousand yards, I'd say that's some fine shooting. Darned fine shooting, indeed."

***

EPILOGUE

A NEIGHBOR LOST his oldest son that day. Landon Reid lost two deputies, a man and a woman. They were buried with full honors. Only one had a family, which continues to receive death benefits from the state's insurance fund set up expressly for such contingencies. Five others were wounded, but returned to duty after a full recovery.

Mitch had to have a few of stitches, a brace on his ear where the cartilage had been damaged, and a bandage on his head to keep the braced ear immobilized. Milo had two cracked ribs, some bad bruising, and some cuts that needed suturing. So did Landon. Jessie suffered a bruised knee, shoulder, hip, and shin along with a badly sprained ankle from drop rolling on the rocks as Barry shot at her. She suffered a shoulder dislocation from Landon dragging her, plus a broken arm, some very sore ribs, and a great deal of bruising over most of her torso from Landon's crushing body slam.

Both Acer and Jessie had to have casts, Jessie on her right forearm, and Acer on his right front leg. Acer had a hairline fracture of the ulna. Jessica had breaks to both the radius and ulna. Landon and the dogs all had cuts and burns from the rain of burning debris, but all of it was much better than dead.

The crushed, broken, and burned remains of Barry Olmstead were extracted from beneath Landon's unit, and, after autopsy, sent to the crematory, then deposited in the county's version of Potter's Field when no one came forward to claim his body. Oli Anderson's bullets, which had gone right through Barry Olmstead's shoulder and head, were never recovered. No one bothered to look for them.

Motive for the murders was never confirmed, but interviews with family and friends conducted by FBI profilers began to suggest that Barry might have been sexually abused. He was known to have been badly bullied by an older sister, a sister whose whereabouts are still unknown. As a teen, Barry exhibited voyeuristic and manipulative tendencies, inducing friends and fellow students to execute acts he planned and observed, but in which he did not often participate.

Six Canadians were identified among the deceased. The rest came mostly from out-of-state, with only nine local victims. All deaths of the victims found on Long

Peak, save one, were able to be attributed to Barry because of a macabre diary found in his safety deposit box. The identity of one of the oldest sets of recovered remains found upon the slopes of Long Peak was never identified, but the body of Flora Roberts was discovered buried in her back yard, yet another victim of Barry Olmstead's perverse legacy. She was exhumed and, after autopsy, given a proper funeral and interred in the family plot at the Northridge Cemetery.

THE END

Would you please take a moment to leave your honest review for me on Amazon? Even a one liner would be appreciated, and, if you are interested in knowing when new books and audio versions of novels in the *The Jessica Anderson K-9 Mysteries* series become available, you can sign up for my newsletter on my website, DLKeur.com. Thank you. –Dawn

ABOUT THE DOGS

MITCH, THE MARVELOUS MALINOIS

MITCH WAS FOUND on the streets on Miami by ABMR (American Belgian Malinois Rescue) in October 2017. They guessed that he was born sometime in July.

In November, he went to his foster home in Orlando. His foster mom is a police officer at the Orlando Airport and her K-9 is a bomb specialist.

Ann's daughter saw Mitch online, and Ann Davis asked to adopt him, which resulted in an intense series of interviews and a home visit. Says Ann, "It was like I was adopting a child. They agreed to let us adopt Mitch and his gotcha day was officially February 2nd."

MILO, QUEENIE, OSO, ACER, AND THE REST

MILO IS MODELED after my beloved Bailey. And, yes, he really was that elegant and tall. A wonder mutt, Bailey, for me, was extra special. I so wish he were still with me.

Queenie is based on an Irish Setter I inartfully nicknamed 'Red'. She was a windfall who wound up going on to win all sorts of awards, both for her conformation—the judges drooled over her, in fact—and for her startling skills. This dog had a soul of boundless joy and was responsible for finding a lost six-year-old.

Oso, the Elkhound, was a dog I had as a kid, and, yes, I named him Oso, because he looked like a fuzzy bear. He wandered in one day in the middle of winter, starved and sick. We took him in …as we did all strays, got him the veterinary help he needed, nursed him back to health, and kept him. Ultimately, because he was an Elkhound, a breed known for their air scenting skills, he was responsible for finding people lost in an avalanche in our mountains during Christmas break one winter. His very best friend was Erasmus, the Philosopher Piglet, my pet piglet that grew into a thousand-pound Yorkshire boar. Their friendship lasted their lifetimes, the two of them dying within weeks of one another.

Acer, Britta, and Sumi are all based on various German Shepherds who I have known or who have been part of our family throughout my life. Within these novels, you'll get to know them all and more, along with other notables ...like Chauncey, the Briard ...but that's another story.

D. L. Keur

*

ABOUT THIS SERIES

THE JESSICA ANDERSON K-9 MYSTERIES began life near the end of November 2020, during the Covid-19 pandemic which reference I have purposely omitted from the stories, because, like all of us, I hope to put that behind me and begin, once more, to live a more normal life.

I have a series of books planned for Jessica and her dogs which I hope to write and release on a regular schedule for you (and me) to enjoy. And joy is, in fact, the main reason for writing them, for, while there is drama and trauma, there is a quintessential heroism in these marvelous animals. In writing these novels, I wanted to share that joy, inspiration, and unique richness that is a life with animals, specifically dogs, and of living in "God's Country."

Within this book and all the subsequent ones in the series, all the places and events, as well as all of the persons' names, save one (with permission), are completely fictional. That said, though, the bases for the elements of the stories are very real and true to the land, the climate, and, most importantly, to the animals and people who call this great, but often misunderstood, part of rural America their home.

An audiobook of this novel will be available, probably by the end of May 2021. It's recorded at the time of this book's publication and in the process of being mastered. You will find it exclusively on the author's website, www.DLKeur.com/

*

ABOUT THE AUTHOR

AS AN AUTHOR WHO DELIGHTS in writing stories that I myself would want to read, this is the first novel and series of novels that I've written under my real name. For decades, I've cloaked my identity under pen names, even once deciding to self-publish instead of continuing the traditional publishing route. Convinced to by another author who has become a close friend and writing confidante, I decided to unveil my identity and allow readers to connect me with some of my fiction work.

Writing is my passion. Though, among other things, I'm an artist and musician, writing novels is where I lose myself in The Zone, immersed for hours, even, days, into the worlds that birth themselves in my brain to emerge out my fingertips. May you enjoy the results of my creative travels as much as I.

Dawn Lisette Keur

OTHER BOOKS BY D. L. Keur

Writing as E. J. Ruek

To Inherit a Murderer, paranormal suspense, set in N. Idaho, this is the story of a godmother saddled with guardianship of her deceased best friend's son, a twelve-year-old who is a murderer. (Controversial)

Old Hickory Lane, the story of an Idaho veterinarian

Created Evil, mythic epic fantasy. Get ready for a whole different take on the Apocalypse.

Slightly Disturbing Stories, a nerve-tingling anthology of short stories that end well for the innocent and good. They will stick with you, each a slightly disturbing ripple in your memory, because it's not what's shown or told; it's what's left unsaid that echoes ...forever.

Writing as Aeros

A Gathering of Rebels by Aeros, a 2 volume Science Fiction epic space opera in the most classic tradition of Frank Herbert.

[Title Withheld] (pending publication)

Writing as C. J. "Country" James

Through Better & Worse, a Montana Love Story, Western Family Saga/Romance by C. J. "Country" James

To Have & To Hold, a Continuing Montana Love Story, Western Family Saga/Romance by C. J. "Country" James

Writing as D. L. Keur

The Jessica Anderson K-9 Mysteries

1. *Death Scent*
2. *Lost Trouble*
3. *Title Pending*

How to Write a Good Book in 17 Days, Get-it-written self-help for serious writers by D. L. Keur, non-fiction

Dawn's Flute Notes, Practical Advice for Flute Players from Practice Room to Stage by D. L. Keur, non-fiction

All of them are exclusively available at Amazon everywhere in the world.

And, in Joy, I hope we meet again.

***

Made in the USA
Coppell, TX
07 May 2025

49109613R00256